HORROR GEMS

Volume 4
Seabury Quinn
and others

Edited by
GREGORY LUCE and LEANNE WRAY

I0541437

ARMCHAIR FICTION
PO Box 4369, Medford, Oregon 97504

For more information about Armchair Books and products, visit our website at…

www.armchairfiction.com

Or email us at…

armchairfiction@yahoo.com

FROM SKEPTIC TO BELIEVER...

This collection of bizarre to fantastical tales will keep you on your feet. Or, perhaps, on your back. Remember, fellow horror aficionados, fortitude is a most powerful asset when dealing with the dead...

A short look at our stories:

Art. What exactly is it that holds a portrait so dear to one person and not another? In "Room with a View" and "The Golgotha Dancers" you may find that the phrase "this piece speaks to me" can have several different meanings...

Beautiful naked women and sea creatures abound in the brooding "Vampire of the Deep." But all seafaring chills are put aside in "I'm Looking for Jeff," an eerie account of spectral discord.

"Terror on the Telephone," "A Handful of Dust," and "Dark of the Moon," remind us that we are but a cog in the machinery of life and there really may be things bigger, badder, and bolder than man...

TABLE OF CONTENTS

DARK OF THE MOON

By Seabury Quinn

A woman of incredible beauty, of monstrous evil ...

A HISS like steam escaping from a seething kettle sounded, and Baxter jerked back just in time to miss the vicious stroke of the cottonmouth. Had the reptile not been numbed with the night's chill and torpid with the mice it had gorged at the entrance of the muskrat house it would have been a thought quicker and fleshed its fangs in his hand.

Baxter shivered as he made a detour of the mounded musquash houses, stepping warily about the pools of stagnant water that pockmarked the treacherous surface of the *flottante*. If only he could reach the open water, where the pirogue was moored...there was a bright moon, that would help, but he must beware of the *congos* and the 'gators—they could pull a man down to sure death in the swamp-water.

For hours—for days, it seemed—he had been struggling across the false-land of the *flottante,* every step an inch above death in the stagnant waters of the *lac,* with death from grasping teeth or poison fangs all round him. A *flottante* is a floating stratum of decayed and rotting vegetation resting on the surface of a backwater that has become blocked with storm debris and on which the jungle has set up outposts. Light-stepping, nimble men can cross its treacherous surface, skimming from one relatively solid point to the next before the spot beneath them sinks under their weight, but if the traveler breaks through there is no help for him. Baxter felt the water oozing in at his boot top, and took an agile, long step, landing on an earth-encrusted square of almost solid mat, and drew his sleeve across his sweat-streaked face. If he could hold out...if the moon kept shining...

Three months ago—it seemed a lifetime as he looked back on it—he had been riding from 'Pelier with dispatches from Colonel Cosgrove to General Butler. They'd warned him to be careful when he passed the *chênière*—the ridge of live-oaks growing by the marsh. Three couriers had set out for New Orleans after dark in the past week, and none of them had reached headquarters. News of Mumford's hanging had blazed through the bayou country like marsh-fire, and while the city smoldered in a sullen calm beneath the watchful eyes of provost guardsmen, open season had been declared for Yankees in the swamplands; every trapper's hut concealed a gun, and men who could bring down a squirrel from the top of a live-oak did not waste a second bullet on lone riders.

He should have left 'Pelier at five o'clock and so reached the city by twilight, but there was a girl at the *'berge*, a black-haired wanton named Solange Dufour who craved pleasure *coûte que coûte*—at whatever cost. So he had lingered over rum punch and innumerable *vins de murs*—blackberry wine—till the sun dropped like a shot bird in the west and storm-dark dusk lay over everything.

The dirt road wound and crept along the river brim as torpidly as a frost-stiffened snake, and the *flottante* was knee-deep in a gray haze of dank brume when he reached the *chênière*; the live-oaks with their trailing beards of gray-green Spanish moss came right down to the highway, stretching gaunt boughs up to share dark secrets with the darker sky, and with a prescience of disaster Baxter set spurs to his horse and leant down almost to the beast's mane in an effort to present as small a target as possible.

The wind from the slug nearly knocked his kepi off, and almost as he felt the hot draft on his cheek he heard the *spang* of the Spencer. The horse almost leaped out from under him as he drove his spurs into its flanks. He saw the carbine's flash in the deep undergrowth and heard the whip-crack of its report just before he felt the numbing impact of the ball in his left shoulder, felt his arm go dead, and knew he had been hit.

The next thing he remembered he was laying on a pallet and a warm spoon pressed against his lips. The smell of soup was in his nostrils and a soft voice crooned, "Drink it, beautiful young mans, drink it for Doudouce; it will be a *remède* for you. *Mais out. But certainly.*"

The soup was hot and very good, *gombo filè*, made with several kinds of fish and shrimp and crabmeat, spiced and thickened with chopped sassafras leaves and piquant with strong wine. He felt his strength returning with each spoonful, and looked about him with that feeling of luxurious laziness that only convalescents know. The woman, who knelt by him and supported his head in the bend of her left elbow, was like something seen in a dream from which he had no wish to waken.

Her face was narrow with an arched, thin nose and high cheekbones beneath which delicate hollows showed; her great brown eyes beneath their drooping lids and haughty brows were soft and gentle as a gazelle's; her lips were full and sensuous and darkly red, like the darker kind of strawberries. Her skin, untouched by color, seemed to have been dusted with fine grains of powdered gold and the hair that hung unbound down to her shoulders was the purple-black of a grackle's throat and held a heady perfume of suave spices in its shadowed depths. Great golden crescents dangled in her ears and round her throat was looped a necklace of gold coins, American half eagles, British sovereigns, Spanish dollars, French louis d'ors, even Persian krans and Danish frederiks. Her sole costume was a white-cotton chemise, sleeveless, open to the waist to show a narrow V of golden-tinted skin and the entrancing rondure of her small high breasts, and a petticoat of scarlet woolen stuff extending just below her knees. Her hands were small and slim and very soft, her naked feet most delicately shaped.

"*Bien. Bon.* You feel better now, *hein?*"

She sat back upon her heels and eased his head down to the husk-stuffed pillow. "*Hé,* you were *malade á la morte,* you, when I first found you, me."

He managed to contrive a grin. "Where did you find me, you?" he asked in imitation of her Cajun dialect.

"*Cré nom!*" she spread her hands and raised her brows and shoulders, "in my *basse cour*—how do you call him?—back yard. You had been shooted in the shoulder and were weak from the lost blood when you came creeping *ventre à terre* like the 'gator to my place. Yes. And afterwards you had the *frisson* and the fever. Oh, I tell you, you were one sick, beautiful young mans, but me, I cured you of your *maladie,* and now"—she said it simply as she might have stated she had bought a pig or calf "—now you are mine, *m'ami;* all mine." She bent forward and kissed him.

There was little passion in the embrace, it might have been a mother's or a sister's, but there was a finality about it, definite and decisive as a herdsman's putting his brand on an animal.

He learned the story by degrees. The storm that had been threatening when he set out for New Orleans had broken almost at the moment he was shot—one of those explosive deluges when every ditch and gully ran awash at once and the dry, dusty road changed to an overflowing flume... The sniper who had fired at him hugged the wood's shelter, and in the downpour, acting more by instinct than volition, he had crept between the trees and underbrush until he reached the clearing where her cabin stood. The rain that washed his tracks out washed the telltale blood away, so he was safe from pursuit when she heard him whimpering *comme une 'tite chouette*—like a little screech owl—by the hedge of thorn-locust that separated her yard from the jungle.

She had dragged him to the house somehow, though he was *lourdement comme un ours*—heavy like a bear—and cut his tunic and shirt away. His wound was bleeding freely and he was weak from loss of blood, but the bullet had ploughed through the flesh, so she did not have to probe for it, and no bones were broken. She made a pack of cobweb and bandaged it on the wound, and fed him tea of coatgrass—*l'herbe cabri*—by the spoonful when the quaking fever came on him. Then a long diet of milk soup and finally the nourishing *gombo.* Now he was all well, almost, and ready for the *pot-au-feu*—the meat boiled with vegetables.

HIS strength returned slowly, and one day he was able to go out to the dooryard and sit in the armchair made of a sawn out cask and bask in the sunshine. That day she greeted him with a dazzling smile and coming close to him put both arms around him. He would have been sub-human if he had failed to respond to her embrace, but he was unprepared for her ardor, for as his arms closed around her slight shoulders and drew her to him she pressed her mouth against his so fiercely that it seemed their lips must be bruised. The arms about his neck tightened and she pressed her body against his, rigid as a carven thing, then limp and yielding, then once more rigid, and as she groaned softly with a kind of animal-whimper he could see her half-closed eyes go empty of all sight, like the eyes of a dead woman.

Her cabin was a one-roomed hut, not a flimsy frame hung with palmetto leaves, but made substantially of logs and weather-grayed timbers that had been salvaged from the river's flotsam. Its entrance was closed by a door carved with elaborate arabesques and hung on massive hinges of cast bronze, obviously once part of a "floating palace" river steamboat, and the windows were highset and small, so at full daylight there was always lodgement for small pools of shadow in the corners. The floor was hard-packed earth and furniture was primitive, a bed constructed of four stakes set upright in the earthen floor with strands of rope and rawhide lashings stretched between them to support a mattress filled with corn husks, and a chest of drawers, much warped from long exposure to the water, evidently something rescued from the jetsam of a wrecked or burned packet. There was no cellar, but a *magasin* of plastered stones with a sod roof stood in the yard, and in this Doudouce kept her small store of staples: *vin d'orange, vin de murs*—orange and blackberry wine—a few bottles of cognac, some coarse brown sugar and a powder-can of salt. Oranges grew on the backlot, and grapevines clambered over a low trellis. In a clay oven Doudouce baked *croquignoles*—hard, brittle biscuits—and on a grating set above a shallow pit she fried the fish or meat or chicken or boiled the shrimp or crab or brewed the spicy *gombo* and the hearty *pot-au-feu*.

Life was pleasant, indolent, and utterly without objective. The quiet, lazy days flowed by as sluggishly as the brown river sliding to the Gulf. His blouse had been spoiled when she cut it off to dress his wound, but she made shift to mend his shirt, and when his strength returned enough for him to walk and go with her on fishing trips in her pirogue she made him leave his boots off—"You mus' go *pieds nus, comme moimême*—barefoot like me—" she told him. "Cajun peoples do not wear the shoes when they can help it."

"But I'm no Cajun," he protested. "I'm—"

"*Foutre, non!*" she laughed. "I say you are a Cajun now; me, I have adopted you!" and she kissed him again, her head flung back, her lips apart. "Now, what you say, *hein?* You do like I say, *non?*"

Her kiss drained him of all resistance. "Yes, yes!" he gasped. "I'm anything you say, Doudouce. I'm—I'm—"

She put her hands up to his cheeks and patted them gently. "You are a very sweet young mans, *m'ami,* an' me, I love you very much. Yes."

She was in his blood like an unconquerable drug, and like a drug she mastered him completely. At any hour, day or night, she could compel him to her will by a soft word or gesture, almost by a look, and while she was consistently gentle, she was insatiable in her demands. She took all, but she gave all. She cooked his food, washed his clothes, she waited on him hand and foot—sometimes even fed him out of hand, taking food from her plate and putting it into his mouth—but she brooked no denial of her wishes, giving orders as one rightfully entitled to obedience, and expecting instant and unquestioning compliance. It pleased her to weave wreaths of orange blossoms for their hair, and when he protested that such things were "sissy" she paid no more heed to his objections than a mother would to a son's remonstrance against velvet clothes and curls. If he wished to linger in the dooryard after sundown while he smoked a final cheroot she would call him, at first softly, then with an imperious voice, and, sighing, he would toss the half-smoked cigar away and go into the scented darkness of the cabin where soft arms and softer lips awaited him.

She puzzled him. Was she a *femme de couleur?* He had seen white women with far darker complexions, and octoroons in New Orleans with skins far lighter. Still... Who were her parents? How did she come there? She appeared well supplied with money. A linen bag in the storehouse was literally filled with gold coins. Could these be from a treasure trove, the buried booty of Lafitte or Pierre Rambeau or Vasseur? How had she come by them? Did she know where more could be found? When he asked her she shook her head and laughed. When he persisted she came close to him and reached up, drawing his face down to hers. Her laughing lips were cool and moist against his hot, dry mouth and the treasure in his arms wiped out all thought of pirates' buried gold.

Sometimes it seemed to him as if he'd given his soul into her keeping, and somehow this seemed disgraceful; yet why, he asked himself, should he consider it shameful? Except for his extraordinary handsomeness James Baxter was an average young man, thoughtless, fun-loving, rather superficial. Until it passed from his keeping into hers he'd hardly known he had a soul.

He was afraid of her, too. That time she charmed the snake she'd shaken him to the foundation of his being; put an almost superstitious fear of her into his heart. He was coming from the *magasin* with a jug of *vin d'orange* when a rattler sounded its warning right at his feet. To please Doudouce he had gone barefoot, and the snake lay coiled less than ten inches from his bare ankle. If he moved it would strike, and would surely drive its fangs in him before he could leap to safety. Perhaps it would strike anyway so he was doomed if he stood still or moved. The fear of death was on him, nausea crawled in his stomach and clamored in his throat. His breathing stopped and paralyzing numbness settled on his limbs. Then suddenly: *"Hé, labas, M'sieu' le Serpent Sonnette! Va t'en toi, oui!*—Hey, Mr. Rattlesnake, get out of here, I tell you!"—came Doudouce's command, and at her voice the poised head lowered and seemed to listen. *"Tendez, toi, va t'en*—Listen to me, you, get out of here!"

The diamond-shaped, death-freighted head lowered, and the snake slithered away like a reprimanded dog. Baxter breathed again, but with an effort, and turned trembling to Doudouce. "Wh—what are you?" he demanded in an awed voice.

"Hé!" she laughed delightedly and stood on tiptoe to kiss him. *"Je suis tienne au grand jamais*—what should I be but thine forever, my beloved?" she asked, then added, almost darkly, "And thou are mine the same way."

But that had been only a foretaste, the faintest whiff of brimstone from the bottomless pit on whose brim he had been standing unsuspecting.

Last week three strangers came into the clearing by the cabin, lean, fox-faced men with guns held in the crook of their elbows and grim determination in their bearing. *"Hola, Doudouce Boudreaux,"* called their leader, "we hear you have a *ventrebleu*—a blue-bellied Yankee—in your house."

"En bas," Doudouce whispered, and for the first time Baxter saw her self-possession falter. *"Au-dessous de châlit, mon amoureux!*—creep beneath the bed, my lover!"

IT MIGHT have been around midnight, perhaps a little earlier or later, when he wakened to the sound of singing. The moon was round and bright and almost in the center of the sky, but in the cabin it was dark, and when he felt along the coarse rep of the mattress Doudouce was not there, though the place where she had lain was still warm. He went to the high window at the back of the room and looked out.

The orange trees dropped down a shower of petals, but the orange blossoms on the ground and in the air were not whiter than her slim moon-washed body as she knelt and held a clay *bassin* of water up to the white moon. She sang a chant of strange words, words that had been old when Babylonish priestesses invoked the Moon Goddess Astarte. And as she sang the water in the basin frothed and boiled and then fell still again, and as it quieted she put the dish to her mouth and drank greedily. A drop of water spilled from the dish to the grass, and another, and Baxter saw them fall like silver coins among the orange petals, but the kneeling woman drank and drank, and first a little concave hollow showed in the moon's disc, and then a larger one, until the moon was darkened as if it had been wiped from the sky, and presently from far away there sounded a dog's howl, and then another and another, until it seemed that all the dogs in the world mourned the loss of the bright silver sphere at which they had been wont to bay.

There was no moonlight any more, but by the faint gleam of the stars he saw her fall face-forward on the ground and heard the threshing of her limbs as she clawed at the earth. She rolled and fought and struggled like a thing in its death agonies, then lay still, panting with great, laboring, moaning gasps, and suddenly it was not a woman that he saw, but a cow alligator, eight feet long from snout to tail, and gleaming in the semi-dark of starshine like a thing in armor.

The creature struggled to its feet and slithered toward the hedge of thorn-locust that marked the boundary of the clearing, walking high on its webbed feet, not dragging either tailor belly. In a moment it was gone and Baxter stood alone in the cabin while terror clawed at his spine with icy talons.

He knew he couldn't have seen it. Such things one might read of in books of old and evil magic, but in 1862—the Nineteenth Century...?

He felt his way to the storehouse, found a bottle of *vieux cognac,* knocked its top off and drained it. The last thing he remembered as he fell across the bed in drunken coma was his muttered protest, "I didn't see it! It's not so; such things can't be!"

THE sun was up a full two hours when he wakened to a pounding headache and a feeling of malaise. He had a sense the night had been filled with dreams of formless menace; but what he'd dreamed he could not remember. Doudouce...he felt beside him. She was not there. Then her voice came to him from the dooryard where she baked the morning's *croquignoles*. Doudouce...singing... He came to full consciousness as if swimming up out of deep water. Doudouce in the *orangerie* last night, Doudouce drinking the moon and afterwards...! He walked to the door. She was kneeling at the oven, and the glow from the coals lent a quince color to her cheeks. There was a smile on her face and her small, white, even teeth showed brilliantly behind the redness of her lips. He shook his head as if to clear it of a sediment of dread. Doudouce...sweet, gentle little Doudouce...he must have dreamed it all. He'd drunk the cognac before he had that vision, not afterwards.

But later in the morning he went to the orange grove and probed among the sparrowgrass and fallen blossoms with his bare foot. There, where Doudouce had knelt and drunk the water silvered by the moonbeams, he found two little discs of argent metal, bright and hard and shining as new-minted coins and, he remembered with a chill, Doudouce had spilled two drops as she drank.

TONIGHT he had awakened from a vague, fear-haunted dream. Outside the moon was shining brilliantly, but in the cabin it was dark. Dark like a hole. Like a grave. His hand explored the bed beside him. Nothing lay there. He was alone.

Alone. The thought coursed through him like a cold flame. Alone in this dark place, while outside... he heard a sound, not like a person walking, but like something sliding, something creeping sinuously toward the open door. The breath came hot and sulphurous in his throat and his heart thrashed and jerked like a gaffed trout. Who—what—was outside?

He got up, crept across the earthen floor and looked out. The yard was white and still and empty in the moonlight, but its very emptiness lent terror to its aspect. Doudouce…was she…? He walked softly, to the angle of the house and looked toward the *orangerie*. It was untenanted.

For the first time he thought of flight. They'd try him for desertion if he went back to New Orleans, maybe hang or shoot him. What of it? Hanging was a felon's death, and shooting a bloody one, but they were men's deaths, after all. Not like being torn and mangled by a monstrous lizard.

He crept back to the cabin, found his boots and put them on. He'd need them in the underbrush; there might be snakes about. What else? His pistol? He'd been wearing it when he was shot, but she had taken it; he had no idea where it was hidden, and no time to search for it. The thing above all things was to go quickly, before she returned. She might come back in human form, or…his brain refused to form the thought; that way certain madness lay.

He stepped across the doorsill, and almost ran into her arms. "So?" She swept him with a quick, stocktaking glance, and her eyes widened as she saw his boots. "So, you fix to run away from Doudouce, *hein?*" Her eyes were dark and hard and bright with bitter anger, yet tears stood in them. "Me, I tell you you cannot do this! I saved you when your blood ran out and you were dying; when those bad mens came for to shoot you I drove them off. You are mine, *mine;* you hear it? I—"

His voice was hard and gritty as he interrupted. "You're a damned witch!" He brought the word out like the flick of a lash.

She recoiled from the epithet as from a blow. Her great eyes widened like a cat's in the dark, seemingly all pupil and devoid of all expression. *"Bête,"* she spit the word like a curse, *"niais- niais, quisquidis*—beast, ninny, fat-head, pig!" Then with her little, soft hand that had never touched him save in a caress she struck him in the face.

Hot, furious anger flooded through him at the blow. The flame of it raced through his nerves and crashed against his brain. The fear that is akin to hatred and the hatred that is born

15

of fear drove him to frantic, homicidal madness. He seized her by the throat and shook her as a bulldog shakes a cat. Her eyes went wide and wider starting from their sockets with the force of his throttling, and her mouth opened and her tongue protruded. She fought him futilely with clawing hands and kicking feet, then suddenly went flaccid as a doll from which the sawdust had been spilled, and slumped down to her knees, her body bent back limply and her head as loose upon her neck as if it hung upon a cord. He drove his thumbs into the soft flesh of her throat each side the larynx, gave her a final shake and dropped her as he might have dropped a sack of meal.

Halfway across the clearing he remembered. There was a bag of gold in the *magasin*. It would come in handy if he managed to escape. Why should he go back to New Orleans and be court-martialed? Her pirogue was tied up at the far side of the *flottante*. If he could get to it he'd paddle down the river, traveling by night and tying up by day, until he reached the Gulf. Maybe he could find a ship to carry him to Europe. If he couldn't, he should surely find some sort of hideout. Men with ready money were immune from disconcerting questions. Gold stopped curious mouths and prying eyes. *"Poderoso caballero es Don Dinero."* The Spanish proverb had the right of it. "Mr. Money is a powerful gentleman."

THE moon, a little past the full and shaped like a bent pie-plate, put a veil of magic on the *flottante*, striking back pale flashes from the little open spaces where the pools broke through the treacherous crust, and he could see his way almost as dearly as in daylight as he made for the place where the pirogue was moored. He'd have to be more careful going past the muskrat houses, though; that moccasin had nearly got him...

The eerie, astral silence that accompanies moonlight was broken by a long-drawn, quavering cry, the sound of a dog howling far away. Lonely, quavering and sad as the lament of a lost soul, it wound in a thin wailing coil of sound that spiraled up and up until it lost itself, but in a moment it was answered by another, and another.

The shadows lengthened and the highlights of the landscape began to blur. There was something wrong with the moon. Something crept across its bleached disc, something like a cloud that was no cloud, for it did not obscure, it wiped away the moon-substance as rushing water wipes away a river-bank. A strange, eerie duskiness spread over the *flottante*, and all at once the air seemed heavy, ominous and full of threat.

Baxter licked dry lips with a tongue that had gone stiff. Something that was lurking terror coiled in the depths of his heart, the blood churned in his ears and his breath came hissing noisily between his parted teeth.

She wasn't dead! He hadn't finished her; she'd revived and gone to the *orangerie;* now she drank the moon, and in a moment…

He blundered across the *flottante,* and the splashing of his rushing steps in the swamp-water was panic made audible. No time for careful choosing of the way now…he had to get to the pirogue, he had to, *had* to…

Something scratched against the stiff grass of the *flottante* with a sound like scuttering dry leaves. He dared not turn to look behind him, yet… He brought up suddenly. Only half-mindful of the path he chose, he had come to a wide space of open green-scummed water dotted with small islets, all out of jumping distance from each other.

He, wheeled to make a detour, and stopped frozen in his tracks. Walking high, tail raised, jaws opened wide, came an eight-foot cow alligator, and for a long, horror-freighted moment, he looked into a cavernous white mouth.

"Doudouce," he whimpered pleadingly, "Dou—"

Then the monster charged.

THE END

A HANDFUL OF DUST

By Ivar Jorgensen

All people are born of woman. But the sea gave birth to this man—and then disowned his body.

I AM SURE there are things under the sea we know nothing about. Not just the grotesque marine growths nosing cold and blind along the ocean floor. But stranger and far more horrible things; mad nightmare tricks of evolution that would make our senses reel were they but known.

Long ago I saw something of this—when I was a child on our island in the chill Atlantic. My father was a stern, craggy-eyed man who loved the sea and all things about it. But a kind and able man. He built our house with his own hands before Donny and I were born. He put it in a place where the sea beat screaming and boastful against a rock wall on one side, and was a gentle sand beach siren on the other.

With the house finished, my father turned to the gentle blue-eyed girl who was to be my mother and said, "Now we must have our children."

But all this was before the Night. I was seven, then, and Donny, my brother, had blown out eleven candles on his birthday cake. It was a blustery night with cloud banks scudding across the moon, turning the world alternately light and dark and bringing always the promise of rain. There was happiness and laughter in our house. Well do I remember this because, after we opened the door that night, happiness and laughter were gone for a long, long time.

The knock upon our door was a heavy, sullen thud; again and again, in slow lumbering rhythm that made one think of ponderous, unhurried entities.

My father opened the door.

A man stood on the threshold: a man, as we all truly and sincerely believed. Thin spindling legs dripped water and bits of seaweed on the stone. His hips were hardly wider than his knee-span, but at the waist he began to broaden until his shoulders reached the width of the door frame. His arms hung loose, swinging in a slight, even rhythm. His black hair was washed tight down to his head as by rising suddenly out of water. Pasty white was the face with eyes, nose and mouth where they belonged but—but something about them—something wrong, like pieces not put correctly together; like a hastily fashioned mask over things better unseen.

And he was completely naked.

The shock of this apparition appearing at our door turned us all to statues. Even my father, whose courage and resourcefulness had built us a home on the lip of ever-present disaster, could not move or speak.

Only my mother moved. Her arm went out undirected, and Donny and I moved into the protecting circle of that arm.

THE MAN moved stolidly into the house and stood with his arms swinging in the odd rhythm. He spoke. The words were unintelligible. As I remember them, they were, "Gar-garaloop-gar," spoken from deep in the chest and almost without lip movement.

My father vanquished his surprise and closed the door. "Good heavens, man! You're in bad shape." He laid a hand on the naked creature's shoulder. "Martha! Quickly! A blanket! He's freezing to death."

I remember clearly that my impression was the opposite. The man did not appear to me to be in the least uncomfortable, nor in the least embarrassed at his nakedness.

My mother arose and fled from the room. She returned shortly with a green wool blanket. She handed it to my father rather than to the visitor, and my father threw it over the man's shoulders and drew it around close in front of him.

The man looked down at the blanket with that deliberation which was to become his hallmark. His eyes came slowly away from my mother's face; slowly, very slowly, with no change whatever in his expression, he lowered his head, then his eyes until they were focused on the edges of the blanket down his front.

My father said, "There, there, old chap. Everything's all right now. What happened? Are there others?" He thought of the natural thing: a boat wrecked on the rocks, bodies beaten to a pulp by the pounding waves. Disaster.

Quite briskly, he gripped the edges of the blanket together and even guided the man's hands toward holding them. "Sit here, old fellow. Sit down and rest yourself. Martha, food and a hot drink. He needs something hot quickly."

Again it was in my mind that the man didn't need anything. Such are the perceptions of childhood. To me he looked to be in no distress whatever; nor in any emotional upset. From my observations, any shortcomings in the creature would have been covered by one term—uncomprehension. And that, the uncomprehension of some lower order. A dog, a cow, a goat. Not knowing. Not caring.

MY FATHER urged him toward a chair. The man turned his head very slowly until his eyes were focused upon my father, then allowed himself to be placed in a chair at the table.

"You didn't tell me if there were others," my father repeated gently. "Tell me where your boat is and I'll go out and do what I can."

Again that maddeningly slow raising of the head; the creeping movement of the eyes upward; the slow focusing. Again he spoke: "Nosh-noshamoo-nosh."

I looked at Donny and found him looking also at me. This was certainly food for merriment. Suppressed giggles were in order. But the laughter was not forthcoming. Was it damned up by pity or fear? I have often wondered since.

My father was entirely confused. He stood looking down at the man, charged deeply with uncertainty. "Your friends should have help," he said. "If you'll only tell me."

My mother had gone into the kitchen. Now she returned bearing a tray. There was bread already buttered, a plate of cold fried perch, a cup of steaming coffee. She set the tray on the table before our visitor and then stepped back, her eyes troubled.

The man had focused slowly upon her and as she backed away his gaze held, cold, flat, empty; a dead, steady watching as from motionless eyes carved into a granite cliff.

"Your food, man! Your food," my father said, and I sensed an uneasiness in his voice; an uneasiness that came from not understanding.

The same snail-like reaction; the head turning and lowering. Father said, "Martha—I'll have to go and look. This man seems to have cracked up. There must be others."

I ran and brought his wind jacket and cap. He left the house and I saw my mother's eyes following him in sudden and silent entreaty. She clasped her hands together. Then, as the door closed, her arm went out and both Donny and I were in its circle.

The man was staring in rapt fascination at the steaming cup of coffee before him. Now there was expression in his badly-put-together face; a new alertness that had depth rather than movement. His hand came up and moved out with that same spine-tickling deliberation. The hand opened and engulfed the coffee cup.

Reaction was swift. His mouth snapped open and stretched his lips wider at one side than the other in a manner remindful of an epileptic under attack. From the revealed maw there came sound even more inarticulate than before. But more eloquent. A "Ga-a-aw-w-w", full of rage, hatred and pain.

THE HAND moved quickly enough this time, but only to clear the danger zone—to get away from the scalding fluid.

Then it was as though a brake had been thrown on and the former snail-pace was resumed.

His face straightened out slowly while he stared at the coffee cup, raised his hand and licked it with a long pale tongue. Close against me I felt my mother shiver and her arm tightened around us.

The man extended a finger and poked the pieces of fish. He favored us with a look—baleful, it seemed to me—then poked a finger through the buttered bread. He licked the finger and sat for an age, apparently deciding whether or not he liked it. He did. He picked up the slice and pushed it into his mouth.

While he chewed the bread his eyes began swinging in an arc around the room. They traveled until they focused upon my mother.

And again there was a faint semblance of expression. It was as though the man was seeing her for the first time; as though he lived without benefit of memory and any experience, no matter how many times repeated, was ever new.

We stood thus when my father returned. There was preoccupation in his deep frown. He signaled nothing to my mother by a shrug of his shoulders, then said, "There is no craft in sight—no wreckage on the beach. If a boat went down, the sinking was swift and terrible."

The man seated at the table continued to stare at my mother. Father stepped close and laid a hand on his shoulder. The strange head—with hair still shining and cap-like, stuck to the skull—came around until the eyes focused on my father's hand—

"You'll need rest, old man," my father said, but now his voice had lost something—and gained something. Lost its original and natural quality of pity. Gained an uncertainty—almost a muted fear as he drew his hand back and unconsciously wiped it on his pants-leg.

"You have a room ready, Martha?"

My mother nodded and my father assumed a false heartiness. "Fine! Excellent. Come along, old chap, and we'll get you between blankets."

THE MAN came slowly to his feet. He seemed supine, negative, entirely willing to be led away. But as he came to the stairway leading aloft, he stopped and turned and walked back to the table. His flat fish-eyes were on the coffee cup. He reached out with great deliberation. His fingers settled over the cup. He crushed it with an inward, squeezing motion, and the cup became shards of broken pottery, the coffee spilling out over the table. The man snarled—a soft, contented snarl then turned and was ready to go aloft.

Donny and I waited downstairs and it is notable that nothing was said—no words spoken between us. Father came downstairs, my mother close behind him. His eyes were cloudy with thought and all the happiness and merriment was gone from our house.

Mother cleaned up the smashed coffee cup and we all sat down around the table. My mother spoke: "We asked him nothing about himself. We do not know his name or where he comes from."

Deep silence was her answer but she pressed on: "Doesn't it seem strange that we asked him nothing about himself?"

Father replied finally: "Perhaps it is best that some things are not known. Come. Bed awaits us."

Donny and I slept together in a room at the far end of the hall. We were tucked in and kissed—a certain preoccupation in the kisses of this night—and we were alone. We lay silent for a long time; a long time until Donny said, "I dare you."

This I had been waiting for but with the hope that Donny would not speak. I was afraid, but a dare—what could one do?

"I'm not afraid. I double dare you."

We climbed out of bed, opened our door softly. All was silent—night silence. We knew where he would be: in the room to the left of the stairs where all guests of the island slept.

We crept forward, seeking and finding each other's hands in the darkness. We approached the door and I grasped the knob and turned it—opened the door slowly, tensed for creaking hinges. The hinges did not creak.

HE was laying on the bed, naked and uncovered, the blankets having been pushed to the floor. He lay upon his back, in exact geometrical alignment with the rectangle of the bed frame. His feet were pressed together, his hands folded upon his breast. The eyes were closed and he looked for all the world like an obscene entity laid out in Christian reverence for the last time.

The moonlight came in the window to lay a span of white ghostliness across him like a slim, pale banner. I shivered and felt Donny's hand tighten on mine. We closed the door and tiptoed back to our room.

"He's a funny man," Donny whispered. "A very funny man." Then he was asleep. I awoke several times during the night to hear my father's quick, firm footstep in the hall.

The following day was highlighted by two incidents which remain in my memory. The man, dressed in a pair of my father's dungarees and a faded blue shirt, was sitting in the parlor staring stolidly into space. My father regarded him from the doorway for a long interval, then came briskly forward. He forced a smile and spoke heartily: "Now I say, old man—"

My father had a fresh pipe between his teeth and had just scratched a match as he stepped forward. The match flamed brightly—

The epileptic twist of the man's features. Bared teeth. A cringing and yet not a cringing—rather it was a coiling of power deep in the pale, grotesque-looking body.

My father stopped as though he'd walked into a stone wall. I saw my father's face as it drained of color, as his hand shook and the match fell to the floor. The man's eyes followed it and my father took a quick step backwards. I could sense the sickness inside of him. Terror? Loathing? Quivering disgust?

I never found out. But knowing my father—his wisdom and courage—and gaining some wisdom myself in later years, I know now that my father saw something in the man that was beyond description. Some lurking unplumbed horror deep in the brain-entrails of our visitor that drove him a step backward, away from its awful stench. Something the learned books of our ages do not contain. Some secret beyond the words we have to reveal secrets.

Father went in to the kitchen and we followed. My mother saw his white and straining face. "We must have help," he said. "I will signal."

Mother nodded and my father retired to the tower he had built upon our house to make use of the white flags—our only means of communication with the shore.

He returned to the kitchen to say, "The waters are high. No boat can come now."

This frightened my mother more than she was willing to reveal. "How soon?"

"Three days I would say. Maybe sooner."

Mother went quickly about her work so her face could be turned away.

THE SECOND episode occurred late in the afternoon. The man had left the house to wander about the island. All morning he'd stared at my mother until she was quivering from flaming and terrorized nerves. Then he had walked out the door.

How he got back into the house without being seen I do not know. Donny and I were in the living room mending the wheels of a broken train when we discovered his presence. A sudden cry from aloft. My mother's cry. A moaning from her lips just before she came running down the stairs.

I saw her face and knew the definition of terror.

She ran on into the kitchen and we followed. She stood clinging to the edge of the table, her throat working in agony.

Then we heard the slow, doomful tread of heavy footsteps on the stairs.

He was coming down.

"In God's name," my mother whispered. "In God's name!" and this was a prayer, but I don't know whether it kept the man from entering the kitchen or not. He stopped in the living room and when I peeked a few moments later he was seated in a chair staring at the wall.

"Don't tell your father. Don't say a word about this. Help is coming. Everything will be all right."

We honored our mother's request, which was not a difficult thing to do because there was little we could have told father. There was so little we knew with our children's minds.

But children can know terror.

My father killed the man that night. It was after a tense and fear-fraught time while the evening meal was eaten and the sun pitched down behind angry seas on the far bow of the horizon. Of the killing I can tell little as there is very little I know.

Mother was aloft and we, busy with our games, had lost track of the man. The signal for tragedy was the slamming of the outer door by my father. As it echoed there came a scream of stark terror from aloft. My mother's voice, shrill and primordial as the scream of the defenseless woman in the dim dawn of time.

My father leaped through the living room; his feet did not seem—to our startled eyes—to touch the floor. Only his hand touched the wall, to come away gripping the rifle that sat on wooden pegs driven into the beams.

DONNY and I waited unable to move. Again the scream came and under it, as though supporting it in a duet of macabre music, came slavering gutturals: "Glag-glagamoo-glag."

Then the roar of the rifle. A thudding weight on the floor aloft. The weeping of a woman.

We climbed the stairs, Donny and I, when our courage was sufficiently girded. We saw our mother on the bed. Father was kneeling beside her, stroking her hair.

On the floor in the hall lay the man, again naked, and now with a gaping chest from which oozed a blackness I knew—in later years—was not blood.

A semblance of cold normalcy was restored—deliberately forced by our parents who had the responsibility of children in their house. But our questions were greeted by silence and soon we stopped asking.

We were allowed up far later than usual that night, staying close to the warm glow of the lamplight which seemed to throw out a protective encirclement against the grisly silence and darkness of the stairwell leading aloft.

And came the moment when my father arose from his chair, took one of the lamps, and ascended the stairs. We waited and after a long time he came down. He stood holding the lamp high, and in his face we could see him as we had known him before; the pallor gone; the fear blown from his eyes; the heavy pipe held serene between his teeth.

"I think you should all see," he said. "I think you should come up with me."

Donny and I were eager for the chill adventure. We went aloft single file, the lamp-circle pushing back the darkness.

Into the room where my father had placed the body.

And it was a perplexing thing, what had transpired upon the body.

It was vanishing—shrinking and becoming nothing under the sheet with which my father had covered it. His face and the face of my mother were abrim with questions unasked and un-answered.

But the terror and the loathing and the balancing on the rim of insanity were gone. There was nothing here. Only some curious covered thing shrinking away beneath a sheet.

With an air of abstract investigation, my father lifted the sheet. My mother caught her breath but said nothing.

The form was already gone. Only a disagreeable mass remained and, as we watched, that too seemed to shrink and become less than it had been before. Father dropped the sheet back into place and we filed downstairs.

UPON THE following day—we had been forbidden the second floor—my father went aloft shortly before sundown. He returned to the living room carrying something in his hand covered by a towel; a small something that scarce burdened his palm.

"Come," he said.

We went with him out of doors, to the pounding side of the island where we stood upon the rocks and watched the sea beat and reach up toward us.

My father extended his hand out over the lip of the rock, turned it palm down and drew back the towel.

Something fell down and down into the water. Like a handful of wet ash; like a scraping of refuse taken away in order to make some small place cleaner.

"It came from the sea," my father said. "And to the sea it must be returned."

He wiped his hand on the towel and we returned to the house he had built for us there on the edge of the deep and unknown ocean.

As we were about to enter, he stopped. "Nothing more will ever be said about this. It is over. Done with. We will never speak of it again."

And we never did.

THE END

TERROR ON THE TELEPHONE

By Lee Francis

*What mad—and monstrous—thing had control of the High Junction
telephone exchange's machinery?*

THIS account is presented in part by Doctor Jean Medeor of
High Junction, Colorado and made complete by the diary of
Frederick Cool. Doctor Medeor is no longer alive to present
what proof she may have had of its truth. I am too tired and
shocked to care whether or not the medical profession believes.
Frederick Cool is also gone, yet the painful scrawl of his last
weeks present a picture too pitiful to misbelieve and too
fantastic to dare accept as the whole truth. It is the picture of a
man dying the worst imaginable type of death. For Frederick
Cool's brain was stolen and he died insane. Do I confuse you?
Listen to Doctor Jean Medeor's letter written in the early Fall of
1944:

Doctor Peter Fromm
235 Trust Building
Fresno, California

Dearest Peter:

I told you that it would be hard to stay in High Junction
this winter. I'm lonely for those cloudless, warm skies, and for
you. I'll stick it out, for I know that a young doctor, and
especially one of the weaker sex, doesn't get a chance to hang
out her shingle every day.

High Junction is up here on the Divide where it gets snowed
in sometimes for several weeks. The temperature drops to thirty
below and shows a strange reluctance to rise again. I'm afraid
I'd rather be Mrs. Doc Fromm this winter, but I decided to
become a career girl, and I'll stick it out.

I *do* have an interesting case. Frederick Cool is his name and he used to run the telephone exchange here at High Junction. I'm afraid he's slightly wacky, Peter. Yet, he's nearly sixty and quite harmless. He has the smoothest face and kindest blue eyes I've ever seen.

Cool came to me three weeks ago. He said he had retired from his job at the exchange, because they had installed one of these mechanical relay systems here for handling telephone calls. You remember the one downtown in Riley Township? A small, brick building, locked up, windowless, with a magic inside that sorts and puts through any call you care to dial? With them, one operator can handle several small towns. That gives you the picture.

Frederick Cool is insane for sure, Peter. I would say, after questioning him for some time that he retains only a vague idea of what goes on about him. I treated him kindly, advising him to get away from High Junction and take a vacation in a more friendly climate. He had a temper tantrum and wanted to know what a woman doctor would know about that. Threatened to change doctors. I reminded him that I was the only one in town and he calmed down a lot.

He said he was sorry, and that there was something that I ought to know about. I'll never forget how the poor old man affected me. It was a cold, unfriendly day to begin with, and a first snow had placed a wet blanket on everything, including my state of mind. Cool leaned forward and said:

"You see Doctor, I know I'm crazy. That's unusual, isn't it? Most insane people think that they are normal. *I know better, and I know why.*"

His words were spoken hardly above a whisper.

"I haven't told anyone," he continued, "and I'm not going to tell you. My mind isn't clear now. I couldn't remember all the details, so I wrote them down."

HE WAS wearing an old tweed suit with frayed cuffs, and trousers neatly patched at the knee with a slightly different colored fabric. He brought from his inside coat pocket a collection of papers. They were as many as the colors in Joseph's coat—pages torn from magazines with notes made in the margin-sheets from nickel scratch pads.

He passed them to me and ducked his head as he spoke, as though talking to the floor.

"I'm ashamed of the condition of my diary. I wrote when I could—when my mind was clear."

Truthfully, Pete, I didn't want to read the stuff. I couldn't hurt his feelings.

"I'll keep this in my desk," I promised, "and read it when I can. Perhaps it will give us a basis for treatment of your case."

That ended our conversation. He wandered out into the street and down past the new telephone building. It's a small, fifteen foot affair with a freshly painted, locked door. Inside, the mechanical 'operator' takes care of the job Cool used to take so much pride in. Cool hesitated opposite the building, then as I watched him, he shook his head slowly and went shuffling onward.

I didn't have time to look at the diary until the following Thursday. Then, as I expected Cool in on Friday, I scooped his papers from my desk, dropped them into my bag and took them to my hotel room. My room is very lonely, Pete. I guess I've mentioned that in every letter. I'll be very happy when I've proved to the world that I can be a good doctor, and have the chance to settle down and prove that. I'm just as good a wife. Do I bore you, future husband?

Finally I put my bare feet on a hot water bottle, picked up Frederick Cool's strange manuscript and started to read. I intended to put it aside in twenty minutes. When the Central--Divide freight came through town at three this morning, I was still reading. Pete, I'm going to say the same thing that Cool did in my office the other day.

I'm ashamed of the condition of the diary. Cool wrote only when his mind was clear. He didn't write well. I tried to read with a cool, scientific approach. Now I'm exhausted and all tied up inside. I'm not at all sure of my own sanity. I'm sending the diary to you because it has given me a queer, lopsided viewpoint on life. Perhaps the intense cold has affected my brain. *Perhaps I'm going crazy.* You're the only one I can depend on. I've always come to you when I couldn't plan for myself, and you've never let me down.

You're so far away from this icy bit of Hades, perhaps you can read with a clear mind. I want your clear, honest opinion of Fred Cool's manuscript. I'm only sure of one thing now. When I pass that tightly locked phone building on Main Street, I stare at the windowless walls and wonder if strange death lurks within the sealed crypt. For Heaven's sake, don't tell me I'm mad until you've read every last word.

I love you, Doctor, in case you've forgotten.

Jean.

The diary was in bad order when I started to assemble it. I became so fascinated by the worn pages that I asked my secretary to transcribe them at once. She worked on them as I read and soon the whole story was assembled in some order and ready for study. For some time, I wondered if a trip to High Junction would be necessary. It would be a good excuse to rush to Jean's side. However, we had both decided that we must live alone, at least until we could convince Jean's father that her study at medical college had not been wasted time and effort. We hoped that once she had proven her worth to High Junction, the old man would bless our marriage and accept me as a son instead of a rank impostor.

It was a difficult decision, but I knew that I must stay away from Jean as long as I could. We would weaken easily if fate threw us together much oftener. We planned to marry in the Spring.

Perhaps, also, the diary of Fred Cool had the power to upset a man's thought processes, until the reader felt that he might be slightly mad to accept the material he found on those pages.

Perhaps I, like Jean Medeor, wasn't able to think clearly after reading so unusual a story. You may judge.

Doctor Peter Fromm
Fresno, California

THE DIARY OF FREDERICK COOL

MY NAME is Frederick Cool. I am an old man now, yet not old judged by normal standards. I am done with life. Even now I am dead. Dead as surely as though someone held a knife at my throat. More accurately, my brain is being dissected bit by bit, and placed in another receptacle, prepared for it long ago. It will go on functioning, yet it will not be mine. My brain is helping a killer. A killer so powerful and so subtle that no one recognizes it or is able to prepare for war against it.

Let me tell you why I die without a brain, without knowing much of what goes on about me—or caring.

Twenty years ago I rode into High Junction in an empty freight car bound for California. In those days, three engines puffed up the mountain, dragging their heavy trains over the hump. I was young then, disowned by my family in England and recently arrived in America on a tramp steamer. I stayed in High Junction. I hadn't planned to do that, but a yard detective found me, half-frozen, jumping up and down beside the freight trying to warm myself. He warned me to get away from the train and foolishly I tried to quarrel with him. I awakened in jail, a hard lump on my head where he had hit me with his billy.

A sheriff with a walrus mustache warned me out of town in twenty-four hours—"or get yourself a job."

My last dollar was gone. I went to work for the High House, a two story, shingled affair, where I got three dollars a week and a small room beneath the stairs where I could sleep. Those first years were hard. Somehow, High Junction got into my blood. I would lie quietly on my bunk at night, listening to the freight trains as they puffed over the Divide. I would listen to the thin, high scream of the train whistle and the howl of the north wind, and somehow, I knew that I'd never go beyond this place. I hated it, and yet it was home. Perhaps I didn't hate it at all. It had a power that kept me from going on.

I worked for the railroad, laying ties for a spur line up to the mine. I worked one summer, deep in the mine.

Then, at last, I had a steady job.

The job wasn't important to the world. It was very important to me. The day I walked into the dusty loft above the General Store, I was as proud as a king looking for the first time at his throne.

High Junction depended on the "valley" for everything. The "valley" was Denver. If a woman needed a doctor—if the hotel needed supplies—anything—they phoned the "valley" for help. The Mayor called the "valley" for a sheriff to come up after a murderer.

Every call—every bit of business transacted with the "valley" had to go through my office. I ran the telephone exchange.

I thought I was the most important person in High Junction. Once we were snowed in for a week. I walked a mile through waist deep snow and found the break in the wire. I made contact with a portable phone and asked for a doctor to come and see Mayor Wiggins through a spell of the flu. Doc Deverish came. He had to leave the train three miles down the pass and ski from there. He saved Wiggins and the Mayor gave me a gold watch for doing what I did.

"You saved my life, Fred," he told me. "I was about ready to kick off my boots and give up the ghost."

Yes, I was very important to High Junction in those days.

IN LOOKING back across the years, I see many things clearly that at the time were confusing to me. I recall the first time I felt cause for alarm, and how it affected my entire nervous system.

I had been alone in the office all evening. It was well after midnight, and few calls were coming through. To some, the loft would have been a lonely place. To me, it was home. I had a small stove which kept me warm and brewed my coffee. I decided to close up for the night, and was banking the fire when the warning light flashed on above the switchboard.

No one was formal on the telephone in those days. I put the speaker over my shoulders and spoke.

"Yes—who is it?"

I thought I could recognize any voice in town, but I wasn't familiar with the cold, impersonal voice that spoke now.

"This is you, Fred Cool," it said. *"Just testing."*

Someone must be joking, and yet it didn't seem very funny at that time of night.

I chuckled, but deep inside, the voice gave me a start.

"I suppose, then," I said, "that I'm speaking to myself?"

There was no answer.

"Who is this—really?" I asked sharply.

I could have waited all night. There was no reply. I hung up. I was shivering slightly, though the room was warm. The complete strangeness of the voice troubled me. I returned to the fire and drank a cup of coffee. I tried after a time, to convince myself that the whole thing could be blamed on my imagination. It was no good. Then the *content* of the message started to get under my skin.

"This is you—Fred Cool…"

That sounded so damned silly that I decided I was a fool to be taken in by such an un-funny joke. I left it that way.

The next day I was careful not to say a word about the incident. I felt sure that whoever the person might be who had called, he or she would rib me about what had happened. Such an opportunity would be too good to miss.

No one spoke about it. The owner of the voice did not call again—that night.

Those were strange years at High Junction. The town wasn't much. The main road came through here once but they changed the road-bed to a deeper, safer pass over the Divide. It left High Junction a small iron-mine town with a single train that puffed through once a day, weather permitting. People kept to themselves. They went to the "valley" only when it was necessary. Each man was respected for what he was, and not for the earthly goods he had collected. I held a respected place in the community. Not an attractive man, I never married. I lived alone, and I suppose, seemed somewhat of a hermit.

I didn't live what was termed a "normal" life. I ate when I wished, slept part of the time at the hotel and part of the time at the exchange, and came and went as I pleased. Often I stayed up throughout the night, taking care of emergency calls.

I tell you this, so you will realize, as I go on, that I knew how people talked about me. My actions, though strange, are explained entirely by the terrible fear that haunted my mind.

The voice spoke to me again at night, when a thunderstorm lashed at the mountains and lightning splashed its death lights across the water-swept crags. The storm was so violent that I failed to hear the bell ringing and noticed the warning light only when the lightning diminished and the room was quite dark.

I hurried to the switchboard, expecting news of fire or washout.

"How do you like the storm?" the voice asked.

I recognized it at once, though four months had passed since it had first troubled me. I was trembling, but I managed to steady my voice.

"It's—bad, isn't it?" I acknowledged. "However—I seem warm and safe."

I could never capture the quality of the voice. I could never explain it. Yet, I try here, for it was so important to know everything I could about it. If possible, it was a voice like drops of ice water plopping against my brain. It was cold and depthless, yet mechanical, as though recorded in hell.

The hair on my neck seemed to prickle and my heart pounded.

I said:

"Who's calling? I don't recognize..."

"Fred Cool," the voice snapped at me. "You remembered me at once. I could tell by the fear in your voice that you know me. You are Fred Cool—so am I. Amusing, isn't it?"

I was badly frightened.

"See here," I snapped. "I don't think this is funny. Perhaps I'm a poor practical joker, but I don't like this…"

The voice was suddenly very angry.

"It's no joke. You will realize that soon."

DOC DEMOREST decided to come to High Junction. He was an old timer from the "valley." A good man, but tired. He wanted to escape the big town. I went to see him soon after he arrived. He was a sage as well as a medical man. In his dark office, pale faced, bearded and fortified behind a huge roll-top desk, he stared at me with twinkling eyes.

"Sit down, Mr. Cool," he said. "You don't impress me as a man troubled by minor ailments."

I was fifty then. I felt nervous and irritable. Often I forgot to speak to people I had known for years. Didn't even see them on the street, though they reminded me of our passing later.

I sat down a little heavily in the leather chair opposite him. I breathed a little hard and felt tired most of the time. I heard the voice often now. Sometimes I heard it in my mind, even though I was away from the office.

"I want a complete examination," I said.

Doc Demorest didn't move. His eyes weren't twinkling now. He stared at me solemnly, a little sternly.

"You're in good shape, Cool," he said. "Don't start taking pills at your age. Go home and forget it. You'll live a good thirty years yet."

I said:

"I'm not sure. I notice a falling off in vitality. People tell me I act odd. I'm absent-minded and a little—strange."

Demorest chuckled.

"We're all a little batty above the neck-line," he said, and tapped his head with his finger. "I'm crazy as a loon myself, but people expect a doctor to act odd. I get away with it nicely."

Normally I would have laughed with him. I wasn't in a laughing mood. I had to get the whole thing off my chest. It needed telling.

"See here, Doctor," I said eagerly. "I've been hearing voices."

"Lots of people hear voices," he said. "Lots of voices to hear."

I grew impatient.

"I mean a very special voice. A voice on the telephone."

He leaned forward in his chair. He studied me with his bright little eyes.

"Make up your mind, man," he said. "First you heard voices. Now it's a *voice*. Is it a babble of voices or just one voice?"

I felt ill and miserable. I stared down at the faded green rug.

"It's a voice," I admitted. "A voice that doesn't let me rest."

I told him the whole story then. How, ever since that first night, the voice had tormented me. When I finished, he straightened in his chair, searched his desk for a battered pipe and packed it full of tobacco. His movements were deliberate. He was deep in thought. When the pipe was lighted he puffed deeply and stared at the ceiling. Then he rose and went to the window. He came back after a while and put a kindly hand on my shoulder.

"I'm an old man," he said. "You are approaching the boundary of old age. As one man to another, why haven't you married and settled down to a normal life?"

He made me very angry. He was like the rest of them.

"Get married and settle down," they said. "You'll go batty, living alone."

I didn't argue with him.

"Perhaps I should have," I admitted. "You see, I left the only girl I ever loved in England. She turned me down when my family took away my chance to gain a fortune.

"True, I'm lonely at times. Perhaps I envy other men."

I stood up, staring at him, trying to get across what was in my mind.

"But don't blame my present condition on lack of companionship. It's something deeper, more horrible than loneliness."

He nodded.

"I can't understand it," he admitted. "Somehow your 'voice' sounds convincing. I have heard people talk about you. I can't agree with them that you are feebleminded. It's something else. Something I can't quite put my finger on. I'll drop in at the telephone office some evening. I want to talk with you up there."

He opened the door for me when I went out, and I felt comforted by his understanding. I tried very hard that day to speak to all my friends. I was so careful to do so that I heard later that they stared after me when I passed. It was as unusual for me to speak to them as it had been to ignore them. They commented on it.

I was branded as a friendly but slightly warped old character. I did not imagine how much that affected my already faltering faith in myself.

AS THE years passed, I started to imagine impossible things. I talked often with the voice, yet knew no more now than I had to begin with. It always teased me until I often felt that I could stand no more of its merciless company. I wondered if it were possible to divide a man's mind into two parts and create two brains from one. I wondered where that other Fred Cool could be located, and spent hours trying to cudgel the answer from my tired brain. Hidden somewhere in that tangle of wires behind the switchboard was another Fred Cool. A merciless, mechanical Fred Cool who had cold murder in his voice. He was murdering me, bit by bit. Driving me mad.

Doctor Demorest came often. He liked to sit near the stove late at night, after he had escaped his own work and talk about his boyhood in France. I often talked about my early visits to Paris, and because I had learned to love that city, I held a place of respect in his heart.

Though we visited in perfect harmony, I knew that he had another reason for coming. He watched me closely, questioning me at great length about the voice in the switchboard.

"Take my word for it," he said one night, "one day all you people will be replaced by the machine. Mechanical controls will dial the number and get the party. Small towns will not employ operators. One operator will take care of a half-dozen towns and the rest will be done by machine."

I agreed with him. I hated the thought of being replaced and having to leave this dusty, lovable junk room of the past.

I was older now. Older than my years. Though my mind was slow, perhaps even feeble, I handled the switchboard expertly, never faltering, never making an error. I was perfectly confident of being able to handle any number of complicated calls.

That night, the answer dawned on me.

Demorest came up about eleven. We had talked about the wonderful mechanisms to come. It dawned on me that I had been a little hazy and uncertain about things all day. Now, sitting at the switchboard, my mind was as clear as a bell. I had been away from the office all day, and a substitute had taken my place. How could I be so dense away from the exchange, and so brilliant-minded when I was here?

"See here, Doc," I said, "don't think I'm entirely an ass. I enjoy your company very much but I know your real reason for coming here so often."

He chuckled.

"And what does the patient suspect?"

"That you are studying me," I said. "You know that I act queerly. So do I. You're questioning me, watching me—trying to guess just what really is wrong."

He frowned, then nodded slowly.

"I don't know just how to tell you, Fred," he admitted. "But the Town Council wants to replace you. There have been complaints."

That was a thunderbolt for which I was not prepared. I'm not sure that it surprised me, but I am sure that I was shocked severely.

"But my work here has been excellent."

He nodded.

"I know. But you see, Fred, you act like a half-wit when you're in public. Everyone notices it. Fred Beecher down at the store says you're as crazy as a loon. Beecher is boss of the Council."

"Blame it on the headaches," I said violently. "I have them all the time now. I feel like blowing up in everyone's face. I have to choke back my rage and my fear. My head is a roaring, empty box. I can't act like a normal, balanced human, with that monster stealing my brain away from me."

He looked very grave.

"You still hear the voice?"

I started to shiver. My hands were icy cold.

"Not for a month," I admitted. "But—it's there. It's there waiting for me."

His eyelids lifted questioningly.

"Still there, is it?"

I knew I had said the wrong thing. It was an idea that obsessed me. I hesitated to share it with Demorest, but I had no choice now. He was the last person who could protect me.

"I'm crazy," I said. "We'll admit that for the sake of an argument. Doc, I'm sure that there is another Fred Cool."

He leaned forward, eyes half closed. His lips were tight.

"Go on," he said.

"ANOTHER Fred Cool," I said. My lips were dry. "He's behind the switchboard. A brain—a mind—whatever you wish to call him, hidden in the labyrinth of wires. He's—stealing something from me. He's taking my brain. I can think clearly when I'm on the job, because, actually, *I'm* not thinking at all. That monster in the board is thinking. That other self. That's why I feel confident and free when I'm here, and like a hopeless idiot when I'm not."

Demorest didn't say he agreed. He didn't say that he didn't. He sat very still, smoking, staring at the ceiling as he fingered his pipe. The room was very quiet. After a long silence, he arose.

"Come in and see me tomorrow, Fred," he urged. "We've got a big problem to iron out."

As I watched him leave, I knew that I had lost. I had sealed the crypt of my own fate. Doctor Demorest was finally convinced that I was quite mad.

I leaned forward with my head on my arm. I'm afraid I cried. It was very lonely and I was no longer a young man. It's hard to lose your last true friend.

I must have slept after that, still seated at the switchboard. It made no difference. The calls went through perfectly, correctly guided by the monster in the switchboard who called himself Fred Cool.

Many changes took place in High Junction while I was away. Mostly changes for the worse. Main Street shriveled and dried up for lack of paint and no interest in maintaining a ghost town. The daily train came only once a week now. Five hundred people remained, most of them miners, a few old timers.

I was almost a stranger in town now. A town of ghosts, yet to me a place of refuge. Doctor Demorest was dead. He had died a year ago, but it had been five years since I last saw him. Five long years since he had sent me to the state insane asylum. Because society condemned me and because I knew my job would be taken away, I went almost eagerly. Five years of sunshine and kind treatment had turned me into a weak, harmless type who could harm no one, and I was considered a fool by most people.

Jake Beecher, a teamster, gave me a place to sleep in his stables and I earned my keep by taking care of his horses. Old timers remembered me, and they were kind. Newcomers laughed at me. My clothes were not good and I'm sure my expression must have been vacant. I make these notes when my mind is quite clear and I can see these things. It is not often now that it remains clear.

Once I visited the lonely room above the general store, to stare a long time at the old switchboard. It is dead now, its wires twisted and broken, dust laying across it in a deathly grey sheet.

Doctor Demorest had been right.

The mechanical man had arrived. No longer does High Junction have a human operator. In a neat, square brick building on Main Street, a complicated machine lurks in hiding. It has the power to accept calls, sort them quickly and send them in the proper direction. I know little about this wonder, and I have never seen the interior of the building. It is locked and mysterious.

I was able to find a certain comfort in lurking near the new phone building. The windowless walls hid everything from me. Yet, by going there, I am able to recapture some of the old spirit—some of the strength that is gone from my mind.

I know that people notice, and joke about my visits. I heard Jerry Beecher tell a friend:

"Old man Cool is harmless. Before he went batty, he used to run the exchange here. He and that telephone building have something in common."

I wanted to make them see that there was something in that building that was mine. The very brain—the mind that used to be mine—stolen from me and locked away in that tomblike building on Main Street.

It was late Fall. I had worked hard all day and when darkness came, I wandered to the phone building and sat alone on the steps. I was sitting near my own tomb. Sitting in the dark, a man alone, waiting for his brain.

"Hello, Fred Cool," the voice said close to my elbow. I jerked around, startled by its nearness. I knew the voice at once. A shudder swept through me. I hadn't heard it for five years. I tried to get control of my nerves, but it was difficult.

"H-hello…"

There came a sardonic, emotionless chuckle.

"So you remember me, do you?"

"I do," I said.

Another chuckle.

"So Fred Cool remembers Fred Cool. Ironic, isn't it?"

I had nothing to say. Dead silence followed. Someone passed on the sidewalk and stared at me. The speed of the footsteps increased. Whoever it was, was afraid. *Afraid of me.*

"You've been away."

"I suppose you missed me," I blurted out miserably. "Missed the opportunity to grasp all that was left. To leave a shattered, useless hulk."

The voice sighed.

"No," it said. "No, I'm quite satisfied. You see, I have all I need. I knew where you were, for our brain is one. You are me, and I am you. You see, you have all the bulk of the brain and none of the ability to use it. I have nothing in actual bulk, yet all the ability to think. That leaves you a half-wit, while I am a human mind, plus mechanical perfection. A very high quality, Cool. Very high."

I UNDERSTOOD it. A great mind in a maze of wires, unable to act for good or for evil.

"I'm growing tired of this place," the voice said. "These people are so much like insects. Trivial things occupy them. They trouble me for all sorts of futile, silly things. I'm developed for greater fields, Cool. Our brain was a very fine one. You remember that."

"What do you propose to do?" I asked cautiously. I was responsible for this monster. I had to learn what it planned. I had to prevent…

"I will destroy High Junction," the voice said calmly. "Destroy it person by person. Then there will be no use of a telephone office here. They will take me and my complicated equipment to a larger, more interesting place. Perhaps, if I am not satisfied, I will go on destroying."

It sounded impossible. I might have been apt to blame this nightmare on my own warped brain. Yet, how could I? It was my brain that was talking. I wanted to run from this accursed spot and never return. Still, Fred Cool planned these terrible deeds, and *I* was Fred Cool.

I sought information that would help me destroy the brain that was my own.

"You cannot destroy anything," I said. "You can't escape from the building. You're tied among the wires."

The voice was metallic and grim when it spoke its last warning.

"Remember, Fred Cool, that there is always a way. Wait for Winter to come, and you will understand my plan."

A new doctor came to High Junction this week. Her name is Miss Jean Medeor, and she is as lovely as she is kind. In many ways, she reminds me of the girl I left in England so many, many years ago. I'm sure that she will be successful, although I don't know why she chose such an out of the way place to start a practice. She told me that she was in love, and that she wanted to be far away from her lover, as it would prove whether she could be a success or not.

I don't understand just what she means, but when I see her, with bright blue eyes, and a smooth, intelligent mouth that shapes itself into sympathetic ovals as I talk to her, I feel as though I want to cry.

I am very lonely and she makes me relive those first days, when I, also, had so much to live for.

Perhaps it was her youth and understanding. I told her my story, and left my diary with her. I know that in her heart she does not believe me. Perhaps she will when she reads what I have written. I pray that she does, for she is my last salvation.

Winter has arrived. A storm swept down from Canada last night and now the voice will act. I will try to save High Junction. It is my own brain that threatens to destroy it.

THE STORY OF DOCTOR PETER FROMM
MOUNTAIN PASS SNOWED IN
Mining Community Cut Off From World

"A polar front, sweeping down from the Canadian Rockies late yesterday, brought a blizzard that cut off High Junction, Colorado, from contact with the rest of the world. The town, inhabited by approximately five hundred miners and their families, cannot be reached for some time. The railroads are tied up with more urgent clearance problems on the main lines. Phone contact has been maintained and citizens of High Junction report that everything is satisfactory in the community. They say that help will not be needed at once."

I stopped reading at this point, and cold fear swept through me.

Phone contact had been maintained.

Frederick Cool whom I had long ago accepted at his face value, had said that the brain would get its revenge when winter came. Somehow, I knew that this was it. I had tried a number of times to imagine how a telephone relay system could get revenge. How it could harm a town. It seemed incredible, almost laughable, until this moment. Now I thought I understood.

The telephone reported that everything in High Junction was all right. It lulled the fears of the people in the "valley." It made them feel that they need not hurry. That time could be wasted.

Cold perspiration broke out on my forehead. I thought of Jean Medeor isolated up there behind a wall of ice and snow. Jean, fighting alone against—God knows what odds—probably at this very moment trying to contact me.

I hurried back to the office and placed an urgent call. I heard the operator in the "valley" speak to Jean, and then she was on the wire.

Or was she?

The voice sounded like hers—and yet it was metallic, and a little abrupt. Not the voice that Jean would use when we had not talked for several weeks.

"Hello, Peter. I'm so glad you called. I'm all right. I suppose you've heard that we had a bad storm?"

I DIDN'T like that. She anticipated my worry. She—if it was she—was trying to show me that she was all right.

"Jean," I said. "That business about the phone? Has anything happened?"

"Everything is under control," she said. "Don't worry about me."

Mechanical—metallic—the voice of a machine.

"Oh," I said. "Oh, well, I thought I'd better check up on you. After all, I do worry about the girl I'm going to marry. Can't find one who'll accept a poor doc every day in the week."

She didn't laugh.

"Everything is under control," she said again. "Don't worry..."

I hung up abruptly. I swore under my breath. I hadn't talked to Jean. I had talked to a monster. A mechanical, murderous ventriloquist. I sat there for ten minutes, thinking—trying to plan. Then I hurried to the apartment, packed a single bag, put on the warmest clothing I could find and caught the afternoon plane for Denver.

I must have seemed foolish, rushing around the dinky offices of the Central Divide Railroad Company, trying to stir up some of the lethargy that seems to exist when a man wants something done and can find no one to do it. I talked with Jake Punkas, president of the tiny spur line that ran through High Junction. He was a slim little man, partly bald and carrying about that expression of one who could very easily go crazy if one more person asked him a foolish question.

I couldn't tell him why I was here. I could only tell him part of it, and that didn't make sense to him.

"But we've been in contact with the Junction since yesterday," he protested. "There's a good doctor up there, plenty of supplies, and they tell us that everything is under control. What more can you ask for? We haven't the equipment to send up now. In a coupla days…"

In a couple of days…?

I couldn't wait, and I couldn't convince anyone here that I was anything but a half-baked medico who had bats in his brain and was releasing them upon a much too busy world.

I had to get to High Junction at once.

I bought a ski outfit, packed my bag full of supplies and started alone. A farmer took me up the canyon as far as his car would go and dropped me there with nothing but mountains of snow and ice ahead of me.

He shook his head when I said I was going through to the Junction.

"Thirty miles almost straight up," he said. "Don't try it, Mister. The canyon's got fifty foot of snow in places. Slides and stuff ain't to be fooled with. You'll never get through."

When I thanked him and started out, he called after me.

"If you get lost and can't make it, stick near the tracks. They follow the river all the way up. The rescue crew will be through. They'll pick you up."

It was cold. So cold that it crept through me in ten minutes. I've never been good on skis. After a half hour, the scraping of those skis against the snow started a little tune through my brain. It persisted hour after hour, until at last, when I fell exhausted beside the trail, I was still saying over and over to myself:

"You'll never get through—you'll never get through—you'll—never—get…"

They said that it took longer to "thaw me out" than any man they'd ever seen. *They* were the train crew, and through some fortunate incident, they had been able to leave Denver much sooner than they had expected. In fact, the rescue crew left town on the same afternoon I started that hopeless skiing trip up the pass. My heavy clothing had saved my life.

I was still weak, but I had eaten hot soup and sat with the men in the caboose of the train. Ahead of us, a huge rotary plow fought its way up through the canyon.

The rotary broke down time after time, and the crew had to dig away the drift to give it a new hold against the snow. The river left a torn, black line down the canyon and the cliffs rose on both sides, dark and ominous.

We reached a high, flat plateau above the pass. Great peaks flung up their teeth like heads, making a circle around the flat waste of snow.

Ahead of us, where the town of High Junction should have nestled in the valley, there was nothing but a jagged pile of ice and snow.

One of the men swore softly. We stared at each other, our silence conveyed an understood message. Then the old brakeman said:

"They—they said everything was all right. That we didn't have to hurry."

"What's happened?" I asked.

The brakeman turned red, swollen eyes toward me.

"That's—High Junction," he said.

The train plowed ahead slowly.

"I seen the same thing happen in Skinner Pass, 'bout sixty years ago," the brakeman said softly. "Slide came down and wiped out a thousand of 'em in one night. One hell of a mess."

The thin, eerie scream of the whistle announced that we had gone as far as we could go. The snow was twenty feet deep on the level. Ahead—God alone knew how many feet of jagged ice lay piled on top of the tiny hamlet.

IN A few hours, the engine had returned to the valley and brought us a complete rescue crew. Huge shovels worked in the moonlight, digging down to what had once been a town.

I guess they knew it was a useless job before they started. One thing kept them working steadily, throughout that long night, and other nights to come. Somewhere, down there at the bottom, there might be someone—something that still breathed. Up until a few hours ago, they said, they had maintained phone contact with the town. I knew differently, but I couldn't tell them that.

But High Junction was gone. Gone as completely as though the great glacier had swept down upon it, crushing it to the ground.

I couldn't have stayed if it had not been for Jean. I borrowed a shovel and went to work with the men. Spotlights swept across the snow. I worked for ten hours before I could see what once had been Main Street. Fate intervened then, and I found that according to a small map Jean had once drawn of her accepted "home town," that the main tunnel was but a short distance from her office.

I worked without feeling now. My emotions were long since frozen by the cold and the utter horror that was inside me.

At last with the help of my newfound friend, the brakeman of the rescue train, I located Jean's office, and found the broken plate glass with *Jean Medeor, M.D.* painted across it. The roof had collapsed, but near the stove, where we found her, the snow had not crushed everything from sight.

The stove itself was still warm, and she was close to it. Three timbers protected her body from the crushing weight above.

I didn't stay in the room. The brakeman said he would wait until a stretcher came down from above. I found a letter which she had been writing to me when it happened, and I took it out and up to the surface. I hid myself as far from the others as I could, and read it. It was my last contact with Jean, and I wanted to share it with no one.

"Dearest Peter…"

That was the most tender, pathetic greeting I had ever read.

"Dearest Peter:

Fred Cool came to me today. He was exhausted and so frightened that he could hardly speak aloud. Last night he talked again with the voice—the brain. He visited the crypt of death that we so foolishly call the phone building.

I had to go with him—to see what he had seen. I had to stop guessing and satisfy myself as to my own sanity.

I met him at ten last night. High Junction retires early. We were careful not to be seen together on the street. Cool opened the door, for he had stolen a key. We slipped inside.

The storm was growing bad. I'm very much frightened when the wind comes down from the north. It does strange things up here—landslides—houses buried until Spring.

"Nothing to be afraid of," I told myself. "If Pete were here…"

It wasn't what I saw in that building, Pete. *It was what I felt.* In the darkness I could see only the ghostly wires that crossed and recrossed into banks of metal cabinets. There was a steady clicking, and the hum of power.

I *sensed* the other Fred Cool. I had long since accepted the fact that the voice didn't actually exist. It could contact Cool through thought waves, but could not be heard aloud.

Another Fred Cool actually lives in that icy, tomb like place. A Fred Cool that is evil and a monster of death.

Fred Cool was ahead of me in the darkness. I could hear his breathing, as though even then he could hear the brain speak to him. He turned and I felt his hand on my shoulder.

"Go back," he whispered hoarsely. "Go back. I didn't realize. It is too late."

A PANIC seized me and I turned to run. I was frightened as a small girl is frightened on a moonless night. I heard a small, pathetic sigh behind me, but I dared not turn back. Outside, I turned in time to see the door click behind me.

Fred Cool never came out. The door closed before he could escape. I ran back and pulled on the handle. It was locked. I started to pound on the door, half crazed, wanting to help the poor old man inside. I heard a voice purring in my ear. At least I thought I heard it.

"This is none of your business. There is only one Fred Cool now. He cannot be saved."

I must have gone on pounding on that door, because someone came up the walk and spoke to me.

"Why, Doctor Medeor, what's going on?"

I pivoted and stared into the eyes of Mayor Joe Green. He had a puzzled, twisted grin on his face.

I tried to laugh.

"Guess I'm crazy," I said. "I've always wanted to see the inside of this place."

I know that sounded crazy, Pete. I know that I acted the part of a fool, but I just couldn't think straight. I had to say something. Green kept on smiling.

"You sure take a funny way of getting in," he said. "Next time the inspector comes up from the valley, I'll have him show you through the place."

He took my arm and guided me down from the steps. It's no good. Do you understand, Pete? Cool's body is in there. They take me there and they'll find it. They'll remember tonight and that I was there. They'll want an explanation that I dare not give.

I must destroy the building, Pete. The monster lurks within it, ready to strike. They'll catch me and I'll die for the murder of a man who came to me begging for peace. Peace from his own brain.

That monster grew bit by bit, sucking knowledge from a human brain. It hides there, partly wire and partly matter. Thick, clever and murderous. It must die, as I sooner or later will die, for murdering a man whom I tried to help.

That's my problem, and I need you, Pete. Need you more than anyone.

Jean"

THE letter was complete. Her signature was there and the envelope was addressed to Fresno. The stamp had been placed neatly in the upper right-hand corner.

I had a job to do. I couldn't help Jean now. But the telephone building was still standing. The brick walls had withstood the battering ram of ice and snow.

I visited High Junction again that week, after spending a day in Denver. I rode up in a freight car, hiding myself from anyone who might recognize me. The car was filled with empty coffins, going up to the Divide to their rightful tenants.

In my bag I carried twenty sticks of dynamite.

The streets were clear when I came back to High Junction. The buildings were gone. Sprawled, ugly beams were everywhere. Men worked silently by lantern light.

I found the phone building and here there were no lights at all. Fred Cool's brain was alone, untouched, untroubled.

I packed the dynamite carefully into the small ventilation opening near the base of the structure. I broke the last stick and pushed the last of the brown powder carefully into place. Then I thawed ice with my breath and watched it freeze again, a tight seal over the explosive.

The fuse was long, and I was safely away from the place and mingling with the rescue workers when the place blew up.

The explosion rocked the mountains, and as I stared back at the dark, unhealthy cloud that reached into the sky, I fancied that I could see the spirit that hung over the place. It was like a black, fearful cloud of death that faltered and sifted to the earth destroyed, leaving only ashes and bits of broken wire.

There is no more to my story.

I think it fitting that I rode back to the valley in the same car, with the same load of coffins. This time I rode with the girl I loved—Jean Medeor.

THE END

VAMPIRE OF THE DEEP

By Rog Phillips

When he drew in his net, he hoped for a startling catch—but snared a living girl who strangely had been dead for days!

"DR. FRANK Richards?"

Frank turned in the direction of the voice. The man who had spoken was short, rather timid looking. Hardly the type he had expected to see in a small town general practitioner, entirely out of character with his voice which was low and cultured.

"Yes," he said cheerfully. "You're Dr. Nelson, I take it."

"That's right," Dr. Nelson said. "Here, I'll take one of your bags."

"No, that's all right," Frank said hastily. "I prefer to carry them both. They make a better balanced load. Which way's your car?"

He followed Dr. Nelson through the crowded waiting room of the railroad depot. Outside a police sedan was at the curb, two uniformed men sitting in the front seat.

"We're taking the prowl car," Dr. Nelson said. "Oscar Freeman insisted, so I left my own car parked down at the station. We'll go over to the hotel first so you can check in and maybe freshen up a bit. After lunch we can go down and talk to Oscar. He can tell you more about Jack Sprout than I gave you in my letter."

"I had lunch on the train," Frank said. "If you don't mind I'd much rather go down now. My practice in New York is pretty demanding at present. I don't want to stay away longer than necessary."

"All right," Dr. Nelson said.

They got into the car.

"I wouldn't have thought of calling you about Jack Sprout," Dr. Nelson said as the car got under way, siren screaming

54

importantly, "except that I felt this thing was right in your line. I've read your book on the symbology of the psychopathic escape from reality. A couple of your other books, too."

"That's good, doctor," Frank said. "I suppose you've given this Oscar Freeman a sketch of my background so that I won't have to waste any time on salesmanship."

"He's eager to give you a free hand in whatever you do," Dr. Nelson said. "Small town police chief calls in famous New York specialist sort of thing. The buttons popped off his vest when he learned you had consented to come."

Frank smiled at the ramrod stiff necks of the two men in the front seat. Nazi storm troopers couldn't have looked more military in the days of Hitler, and that siren could be heard beyond the city limits in every direction. Perhaps even out to the three mile limit at sea.

"Offhand I'm not so much interested in solving the murder as I am in the mind of Jack Sprout," he said. "I gather from your letter that you and Freeman want me to get below the symbolism in his ravings and get him to confess. If I do that it will be only incidental to the study of the symbolism itself. Oscar Freeman might be disappointed in the results."

"I doubt if that would matter too much," Dr. Nelson said. "Up until this happened Jack Sprout was a very well liked young fisherman, Frieda Thorne—well, I don't think Oscar knows what she looked like, I have a sneaking hunch that if you could hand down some authoritative opinion that Jack Sprout was innocent Oscar would be more pleased than if you solved the murder. He'd be passing the buck to you, if you get what I mean."

The car drew up in front of a building made of dirty blocks of stone the same size as modern cinder blocks. It was a typical police station in a typical small town. Built at the same time as the railroad station way back when.

One of the men in the front seat leaped out and opened the rear door, holding it open importantly. Frank climbed out followed by Dr. Nelson. Frank started to take his two bags out of the car.

"Leave them in, doctor," the officer said respectfully. "We'll take them to the hotel and be right back. Only a minute."

"Thanks," Frank said.

HE FOLLOWED Dr. Nelson into the building, across a creaking, much varnished floor, through a couple of doors, and through a third door on which had been lettered quite ornately the legend, "Oscar Freeman, Chief of Police."

Frank received his second surprise. Oscar Freeman was not the rather oldish potbellied self-important character he had envisioned, but an instantly likeable and cleanly built man not over thirty. When they entered he stood up and came around his desk, holding out a hand in welcome.

Frank reached out to shake hands, felt something was wrong. He looked down at the hand he was shaking. It was a left hand. He looked at Oscar's right arm and saw that it ended with a curved hook instead of a hand.

"Lost it in the war," Oscar said pleasantly.

"If you two don't mind," Dr. Nelson said. "I'll run along. Couple of hospital cases I should look at before office hours. You can call me. Otherwise I'll drop over to the hotel this evening, Dr. Richards."

"WHAT DO you want first, doctor?" Oscar asked when the door closed. "See Jack? Or would you like all the dope on the case up to date?"

"The latter would be best, I think," Frank said. "The slant of a third party is often valuable."

He took a chair and lit a cigarette, settling back comfortably.

"Well," the police chief began, "it all began a week ago. We have a big tourist trade here. Three hotels with a total of a hundred and fifty rooms, and most of them filled during six months of the year. I can't keep track of all the tourists, naturally. I do remember noticing this girl, Frieda Thorne, however. Just one in the crowd in the lobby at the Cove Arms. A striking beauty of a type you seldom see. Skin satiny smooth, so smooth it almost seems it can't have any pores, yet with a healthy color. Lips the same way. Rather full but not too much so, and with the same satiny smooth texture. Lipstick that you would have sworn was a natural unpainted color. And maybe it was. Eyes maybe a little too large for a normal person but just exactly right for her, I thought, 'Boy, that could be for me!' Then I promptly forgot about her. You know how it is, especially with a single man. You see a dozen every week you could fall in love with and marry, given half a chance." He looked down at the hook at the end of his right arm, "But you don't do anything about it. Especially here. They'd turn out to be married, or in love with another guy already, and anyway they'd all be accustomed to living on an income you could never hope to earn enough to pay the income tax on even.

"But I did ask the clerk what room she was in. That's how I know it was her."

"Dr. Nelson said you hadn't seen her," Frank said.

"You're the only one who knows I did except that room clerk and he probably forgot about it," Oscar said. "Anyway, it was two days later that she disappeared. It was an elderly woman who reported her missing. Claimed to be a very dear friend of Miss Thorne's, but I suspect she's just a casual hotel acquaintance of the type that instantly becomes your lifelong friend. You know the type. But she spread it on thick enough so that the hotel took a look in her room and found her clothes all there and the bed unslept in. That was good enough. They called me.

"Well," Oscar continued, "I figured no self respecting girl with a nice body would come to a resort town without a bathing suit, so I looked for one. It was missing. That made it slip into a neat pattern. Girl goes swimming, maybe alone, and drowns. Girl goes bathing, meets with foul play. Corpse lying somewhere along the beach, I send my boys and a couple dozen volunteers up and down the beach for several miles. Within an hour we locate the spot where her swim suit and beach robe and sandals are laying in a neat pile. At first there seems no sign of foul play. Even though the spot is very secluded. It's the kind of a place a girl wanting to take a quick dip in the nude would pick.

"It isn't until I bring the stuff down here that I begin to suspect foul play. Here, I'll bring it out and you can discover for yourself."

Oscar got up and crossed to a safe. He brought out a bundle in a cellophane bag. He dropped it in Frank's lap and went over and sat down again, watching him with a half smile.

Frank stared at the bag. Inside was a folded two-piece swim suit and a bath towel type of beach robe. He looked up at Oscar questioningly, then slid open the zipper. Immediately his eyes widened.

"It smells strongly of fish…" he said.

"I thought you'd notice," Oscar said with satisfaction. "And it wouldn't do that if she had just taken a dip and it had dried out. The only way it could get that strong a smell of fish is if it had been soaked in the bilge water of a fishing boat. And it would take several washings to get it out."

"I see," Frank said slowly, "And I can see how you concluded it must be foul play. And obviously if it were, her things could have been washed out and dropped in that secluded spot to make it seem she had taken a dip in the nude and been pulled out to sea by the tide. It would be the logical pattern for a fisherman who found himself getting into trouble that demanded he silence the girl. In itself probably foolproof."

"LOTS OF murders are foolproof if the initial setup is left alone," Oscar said. "The murderer has a conscience that bothers him, or he thinks the police suspect too much and makes further moves to cover up imagined loopholes, and gets caught. I and my boys made a routine checkup of all the local fishing boats over the next two or three days, looking for signs of a struggle, or blood, or even a corpse, though we didn't expect to find one. No dice. We gave it up as a bad job. There were a couple of fishermen we could have brought in on suspicion to make a case and let the people know we're on the job. But hell, why bother?"

"Then Jack Sprout goes to pieces?"

The police chief nodded agreement.

"I was waiting for that," Frank said, leaning forward and grinding out his cigarette. "Let me know as much as you can remember of how he looked and what he actually said."

"When we were looking over the boats, Jack Sprout's boat was okay," Oscar said. "When I asked him the routine question of whether he had known the girl he readily admitted that she had gone out on a fishing trip with him about ten days before she had disappeared. He wouldn't admit to anything more than that. Claimed he hadn't seen her the day she vanished. But he was the only one of the fishermen who admitted even knowing her. I took it on myself to sort of circulate around during off-duty hours, seeing what I could pick up.

"It was Jeb Turner, the bartender down at the waterfront bar that gave me my first lead. He said that Jack Sprout had come in there one evening and started drinking pretty heavily. He ran out of money and hit Jeb up for credit so he could go on drinking. When Jeb asked him what had come over him that he wanted to get drunk like that Jack told him he had seen something out at sea. He muttered something about a girl in his nets. Jeb laughed about it and gave him credit, thinking Jack had just cooked up a whopper as an excuse for getting himself good and tight.

"That was enough to bring him in for questioning. At first we couldn't get anything out of him. I decided I could do better by getting him drunk again. I released him and invited him to have a drink with me. We went down to the waterfront bar. I kept pushing drinks on him until he was pretty drunk. He was so drunk he could barely stay on the stool before he started talking. His story was rather weird.

"He said he hadn't even known Frieda was missing when he pulled in his net and saw her. She didn't have a stitch on, and was astride the back of the biggest old flounder he had ever seen. She got off its back and climbed aboard. Then she sort of doubled up, pressing her hands against her stomach. Water came out of her nose and mouth in a steady stream, then spurts. Finally she straightened up, breathing in deep gulps like a fish out of water. A couple of minutes of that and her breathing became normal. Then she bawled him out good for catching her and Bullza—that's what she called the fish—in his net. He said he apologized and turned over the net, releasing the big fish and all the rest of the catch. Then without a backward glance Frieda dived in. He watched where she disappeared, and shortly a lot of bubbles broke to the surface. The big fish had been swimming around near the surface. After the bubbles stopped it went down out of sight.

"Jack ran into the cabin and brought out his waterscope. That's a piece of stovepipe with a glass in one end. You stick it in the water and you can see right on down. Through that he claims he saw Frieda swim to the back of the flounder and get on. Then they swam away."

Oscar smiled smugly.

"I brought him back to the station and booked him for being drunk," he said. He became serious again. "I didn't want to book him on suspicion of murder. In a small town that's bad. If you get off people keep on thinking you were guilty."

He stopped talking, watching Dr. Frank Richards expectantly.

"On the theory that Jack was too drunk to think up the story," Frank said thoughtfully, "I can see why Dr. Nelson thought it would interest me. He sensed a basic picture of this Jack Sprout falling in love with Frieda Thorne, being spurned, perhaps laughed at by this superior city girl who considered him just an ignorant fisherman, killing her in a fit of anger and humiliation, shoving the deed into his subconscious where even he can't pull it out, then rationalizing it with a fantastic dream.

A dream he might very likely have had the next time he slept after killing her. It's a rather conventional pattern. Murder. The refusal of the conscious mind to accept the fact of murder. Shoving it into the subconscious and walling it in with symbolism. I think I would like to talk with him now."

JACK SPROUT was dressed in water repellent levis, heavy shoes, and a brown woolen shirt open at the neck; all showing signs of wear. His face, neck; and bare arms had the kind of tan a fisherman gets in his open boat under the sun with salt breezes Whipping at him. His face was thin, the thinness accentuated by the heavy thatch of black hair that spilled over, covering his ears and seeming never to have known any other comb than the careless fingers its owner ran through it to get it back from his eyes.

He looked at Frank without curiosity, then turned to Oscar.

"That was a dirty trick, Oscar," he said. "Getting me drunk and locking me up for being drunk."

"I wanted you where I could find you, Jack," Oscar said, grinning. "This is Dr. Richards. Otherwise known as Frank. He's interested in what you said about seeing Frieda with that fish."

Jack glanced at Frank again, dismissed him with his eyes, then turned his attention back to the police chief.

"Are you turning me loose, Oscar?" he said. "You'd better. There's a storm brewing. I've got to make my boat secure."

"That's up to Frank," Oscar said. "He's the boss here. Came down from New York. What he says goes. If he says lock you up again and keep you there till you rot," he shrugged his shoulders resignedly. "I'll have to do it. If he says turn you loose I'll have to do that. Better be nice to him."

Jack Sprout turned back to Frank with new interest in his eyes. He studied him from under his heavy black eyebrows. He turned back to Oscar.

"So that's the way it is, huh?" he said. "You think I'm crazy. Well I'm not. I know what I saw and heard." He turned back to Frank with a sneer twisting at his lips. "But if your idea of being crazy is anyone who sees something nobody else has ever seen, then I'm crazy according to you, and you'll order me locked up for the rest of my life, I guess."

"Not at all," Frank said. "As a matter of fact, I don't think you *are* crazy."

"Huh?" Jack said, startled.

Frank smiled disarmingly. "I'm more interested in what you saw," he said. "I write books about unusual things like that. Things that sound so crazy sometimes the one who saw them gets locked up because everyone thinks he really is crazy. You might say I'm just the opposite of the doctors that lock people up. There are quite a few people running around loose right this minute that would still be behind bars in some state hospital if I hadn't stepped in and investigated what they claimed to have seen or heard."

"And if I don't talk about it?" Jack asked.

"I hope you will," Frank said. "I'd like to meet Frieda Thorne and her fish. Personally I've always thought fish were a lot smarter than most people believe, I don't see anything fantastic in a fish being almost intelligent when it's as old and has been through as much as this one seems to have been."

JACK STARED at him, his expression slowly altering from contempt and defiance to hope and reserved friendliness.

"You *talk* sense," he admitted. "If Oscar'll turn me loose we can go out and look around. I don't think Frieda will come back, but we can look."

"Why don't you think she'll come back?" Frank asked casually.

"Well, she's mad at me because she got caught in my net," Jack said. "And she didn't like me, really. It was just that I had a boat and could take her outside the bay. It wasn't even the same as ordinary tourists. They look at you like you're a character, but human, just the same as they are. She looked at me like, well, like Mrs. Grant, the rich lady, does. Like I belong to some other race. Dogs maybe."

"You mean when you took her out this last time?" Frank asked.

"I only took her out the once," Jack said. "That was two weeks ago. And that's when I'm talking about. She wanted to hire me to take her out. I wouldn't take any money. I was going out fishing anyway, and she came along."

"Alone?" Frank asked.

"Yes," Jack said.

"What'd she do when you kissed her," Frank said, smiling. "Slap you?"

"I didn't try nothing like that," Jack Sprout said. But his face turned a deep red. Realizing this he broke down, "All right," he said sullenly. "So I tried to get fresh with her. What would you have done, when she climbed out of the water, with it dripping from her, without any clothes on?"

"The same thing, probably," Frank said, laughing. "And if she spurned me I'd probably dream about her and think about her, and wind up wanting her more than anything else on earth. That's the way those things usually work out."

"But that's what caused the trouble," Jack said, his mood changing. "She wasn't mad at me for trying to get fresh with her. She might have let me. She was teasing me, running around the boat. But when I caught her—" He clamped his mouth shut.

"She didn't have anything on when this happened?" Frank said. "She was asking for trouble."

"That's just it," Jack said, shifting uncomfortably. "She wanted me to get fresh with her. It was when I wouldn't that she—" A peculiar expression crossed his face. "She wasn't human. I felt it, I left her there on the foredeck and headed back toward shore. That's what made her mad."

Oscar cleared his throat. "I'm sending you back to clink for now, Jack," he said. "The doc and I will talk, and if he thinks it's okay, I'll release you later in the day."

Frank opened his mouth, then closed it. He saw that Oscar had something on his mind.

Oscar had pressed a button on his desk. A policeman came in. Oscar nodded toward Jack, and watched while the fisherman was led away. When the door closed he turned to talk to the city doctor.

"I think that's the slip I've been waiting for," he said. "Jack's boat doesn't have a foredeck. Just an open hold where the fish can be poured in from the nets."

"Then you think he left her lying in the hold?" Frank said.

"In about two feet of stagnant water," Oscar said, "strong with the smell of dead fish. These fishermen seldom clean that out thoroughly. I think he was talking about the last time she went out with him. I think that's when he killed her because she insisted in flaunting her body before him and fought him off. He killed her, left her in the hold for at least a day while he cooked up a plan to get clear. When he got the idea of leaving her swim suit and robe on the beach he took it off her and dropped her at sea."

"What would be the chances of her body being washed up on shore?" Frank asked.

"Practically nil if an experienced fisherman dropped her off shore," Oscar said. "He'd know the currents and drop her where she'd go on out to sea. "That's why Dr. Nelson suggested interesting you in the case. The only way we have of solving the thing short of finding the body is to break Jack down. And you're the only one who can do that." The phone had rung while he was talking. He scooped it up now. "Yeah?" he grunted. He listened a moment, his eyes going wide. "They've found the body," he said to Frank. "Over on Crab Point."

"WE'LL PICK up Dr. Nelson," Oscar said. "He acts as coroner whenever there's any coronering to be done." He grinned widely at his own wisecrack.

After a ten minute wait at Dr. Nelson's office they got started, taking a dirt road that bounced over scabrock as it skirted the bay toward Crab Point, a neck of uninviting rocky beach jutting out from the mainland to extend better than halfway across the inner harbor, and acting as a breakwater.

Oscar was in high spirits. "This is going to wrap up this case in a hurry," he said to Dr. Nelson after explaining about finding the body.

"I wouldn't be too sure," Frank said.

"What do you mean?" Oscar said. "What more can we ask? The body, the man who did it, and just about enough evidence to prove he did it—with your expert testimony, of course."

"You saw Jack Sprout?" Dr. Nelson asked.

"I saw him, doctor," Frank said.

"Was he as interesting a case as I thought he would be?" Dr. Nelson asked.

"Interesting, yes," Frank said.

The police car left the road and bounced violently over the rough beach toward the shore where another police car and a small group of people were gathered. It bounced to a stop beside the other car.

Oscar opened the door. They got out and went the remaining few yards to the shore. There was a brown blanket spread out over something, just a few feet away from the hungrily reaching waves that washed up. It was a nice day. The air was barely moving. The waves came along toward shore in rolling waves that came up without breaking into whitecaps, thinned out as they went onto the beach, and lingered before slowly going back.

"Foul play all right, chief," one of the police said importantly. He went to the blanket and lifted it enough to reveal the head.

"Gawd! Oscar muttered, staring at the crushed skull, "He must have struck her a dozen times to batter in her brains like that."

Dr. Nelson bent down and peered at the ugly wound. Bits of brain matter were mixed with hair and bone, all washed clean of blood by long immersion in water.

"How long would you say she's been, dead?" Oscar asked.

"Can't say until we take her down to the morgue and I give the body a thorough examination," Dr. Nelson said. He looked up at Frank. "Want to take a look?"

Frank shook his head, glancing up with the others to look at the ambulance that was coming.

"I'll do my looking when we have her down at the morgue," he said. "How was she found? Here on the beach where she is now?"

"I found her," a narrow shouldered man in overalls spoke up eagerly. "She was in shallow water when I saw her, I took off my shoes and waded in, and dragged her out to where she is now."

"Good work, Harry," Oscar said to the man. "I'll make sure the big city papers get your name in the story as the one who found the body." He started to turn away. "Oh yes," he said, turning back. "You'll have to be at the inquest to tell about it, too. That'll be tomorrow morning at ten o'clock. Be in my office about a quarter to."

"I'd like to make a suggestion, doctor," Frank said to Dr. Nelson. "Have the ambulance men lift her onto the stretcher instead of rolling her."

The ambulance driver and his helper were already at the body. Dr. Nelson relayed the order to them. Oscar got into the car. The two doctors followed.

They rode along in silence for several minutes.

"I suppose you'll be going back to New York now that the case is cleared up?" Oscar asked suddenly. "You don't have to stay, really. I'm confident Jack will confess when we confront him with the body. I intend to do that just as soon as Dr. Nelson's through with his autopsy."

"You saw the face," Frank said, ignoring Oscar's question. "Are you sure it was the same girl, Frieda Thorne?"

"Certainly," Oscar said. He looked at Frank curiously.

Frank nodded, a frown on his face.

"What's eating you, doctor?" Oscar said, half humorously. "From your expression I'm beginning to think you doubt it was murder."

"Oh, it was murder all right," Frank said. "Or at least, I should say, she was deliberately killed. But Jack Sprout didn't do it. I'll stake my reputation on that."

"Then who did?" Oscar demanded.

"The fish," Frank said quietly. He shook his head and held up his hand as both Oscar and Dr. Nelson started to protest. "It had to be the fish. That's the only thing that makes sense, and even that doesn't make sense unless—"

"Unless what?" Oscar demanded.

"I can't answer that just yet," Frank said. "I'm going to ask you to postpone the inquest while I send for a certain young lady to help me get at the root of this mess. I'll call her long distance. She should be able to get here by morning. Her name is Helen Cooper."

* * *

"YOU'RE Oscar Freeman?"

Oscar jerked around. It was five thirty in the morning. He had volunteered to meet Helen Cooper so that Dr. Richards wouldn't have to get up at such an ungodly hour. He had watched until he thought everyone was off the train without seeing anyone answering to her description, then turned away.

"Yes," he said, sizing her up hastily. She was a little taller than he with her high heels on. A striking brunette with sparkling blue eyes, a vivacious smile. He decided he liked her. "You must be Helen Cooper," he said, smiling.

"This is going to be exciting," Helen said. "Will I get to ride in a prowl car? You like this town, don't you. That's why you live here." She closed her eyes for a moment, then popped them open again and smiled. "It's a nice town. It has a nice spirit to it. But there's something else here. I don't mean Frank. He's here. I can feel him. But there's something else here too. Let's go to where Frank is. I'll feel safer. It's dangerous, I think. At least it's probing, though I don't believe it's sensed me yet."

She smiled again. More than a little bewildered, Oscar took her arm and escorted her out to the car.

"I think I understand Dr. Richards' saying for me to bring her to him even if I had to use force," he silently decided. "She's the kind that might decide to go window shopping at six in the morning and forget what she came here for."

He was uncomfortably conscious of her presence in the seat of the car beside him as the police chauffeur drove toward the hotel.

She leaned forward suddenly and touched the driver on the shoulder.

"Please hurry," she said anxiously. She sat back as the car speeded up. Turning to Oscar she said, "I feel like I want to go swimming, but don't let me." She smiled again. "It's the *drawing*, and I'm so susceptible to it." She slid over next to him and reached for his hand. "Hold my han—" She looked down at the metal hook her fingers had touched. Her eyes widened. "Oh, I'm so sorry," she said.

It was the first time anyone had ever said that in a way that made him feel good about it.

"My other hand is okay," he said, grinning. He reached over with it and took one of her hands. When the car stopped in front of the hotel he regretted that the trip was over so soon.

"Keep holding my hand until we get to Frank," Helen whispered. "And don't leave me for one instant."

She stayed close to him as they entered the hotel. He felt a strong urge to put his arm around her waist.

"I'd feel much better if you did," she said.

Unconsciously he put his arm around her. Then, "Huh?" he exclaimed. "Are you a mind reader?"

A smile flashed over her worried face and was gone. Suddenly she relaxed. "Frank's awake now, thank heavens!" she breathed almost inaudibly. "Take me straight up to his room. And don't go away. Somehow you have a good effect on me."

In the elevator she stood stiffly erect, a fixed, intent expression on her face. When they left the elevator she turned in the right direction, hurrying so fast Oscar had to almost trot to keep up with her. She seemed to know where she was going, and stopped at the right door without looking at the number. Instead of knocking she tried the knob, rattling it impatiently when it wouldn't open the door.

The key turned in the lock. The door opened. Frank stood framed in the doorway, trousers on, but barefooted and without a shirt on.

He was smiling in a welcoming expression. As his eyes came to rest on Helen his smile vanished, to be replaced by a look of concern.

"It's affected you already," he said, almost angrily. He took her shoulder in his hand and pulled her into the room. Oscar followed, his amazement and bewilderment increasing.

BY TEN o'clock Oscar's bewilderment had increased to the point of numbness. And the numbness was altering to something very close to fear.

The ocean which had always been something friendly to him with its mischievous whitecaps on windy days, its lazy swells on calm days, its violently pounding waves that matched the mood of the weather on stormy days, had subtly taken on a third dimension of sinister depth. He began to sense a nameless horror lurking under its friendly surface. The same kind of formless horror that he could dimly remember imagining lurked in a darkened room when he was two or three years old.

He first caught the feeling when Helen broke away from Dr. Richards and began running as fast as her high heels could carry her toward the waterfront. He had become infected with it from the urgency in the doctor's eyes, the way he had said, "For

God's sake, after her! We've got to keep her from getting to the water!"

They had caught up with her. And she had smiled at them calmly when they firmly led her back to the car. But she had changed during those few moments. When she smiled at him after that her eyes looked through him instead of at him or into him. She no longer said anything. She gave the impression her thoughts were a million miles away.

At the police station when the doctor said to put her in a room where she could be watched through peepholes, with the doors locked and heavy guard at every possible avenue of escape from the room, she hadn't seemed to even hear.

He and the doctor had watched her through peepholes. She had wandered about the room, then sat down on a hard bench, her hands folded across her lap, her eyes staring into space, a quiet little smile on her lips as though she were listening to someone. She had stayed that way. She was still in the same position when he and the doctor had come back after breakfast.

"Ten o'clock," Frank said. "This is what I want done, I want Jack Sprout brought out and placed in that room with her. He's to be told that he's being turned loose today, and all that's necessary is for him to wait in there until you can see him. Then he can go. He must believe that when he goes in there."

"But I can't do that!" Oscar said. "I'm not—"

"Do what I say," Frank said. "You'll see my reasons."

Ten minutes later they watched Jack enter the room. Through the peepholes they saw him stop just inside the door, startled, as his eyes fell on Helen. She seemed not to notice him at first.

He sat down across the room from her, studying her. Finally she looked over at him, her lips parting in a dreamy smile.

"Hello," they heard Jack say. "What are you here for?"

"Oh, I'm just waiting," Helen answered vaguely.

"I'm waiting too," Jack said. "I wish Oscar would hurry up and see me so I can get out of here. I'm anxious to take my boat out."

"You have a boat?" Helen said, looking at him with new interest. "Could I go out riding with you?"

"Uh-uh," Jack said firmly. "That's why I'm in here. I took a girl out in my boat. A week later she disappeared, and they suspected me of murdering her."

Helen stood up and walked across the room. She kept her eyes locked with Jack's, dropping to her knees in front of him, resting her hands on his knees.

"Please take me out in your boat," she said. "I—I like you." She leaned toward him, a dreamy seductive smile parting her lips.

Jack glanced about the room guiltily, then slipped his arms under hers and around her waist, drawing her close. She lifted her face. He crushed his lips against hers.

Then abruptly he was on his feet running toward the door. He pounded on it with his knuckles, shouting to be let out.

"Let him out and bring him into my office," Oscar said to the guards.

He and Frank hurried into the office. They were lounging in chairs as though they had been there for hours when Jack Sprout was admitted.

"That girl in that room!" he blurted as soon as he entered. "She's just like Frieda!"

"What do you mean?" Oscar asked.

"What I was telling you," Jack said excitedly. "Different."

"You mean—*alien?*" Frank suggested.

"Yes…that's it!" Jack said. "That's just what I mean."

"Now do you believe the story he told you?" Frank asked.

"Hell!" Oscar spat. "I believed it two hours ago."

"We're going fishing with you in your boat, Jack," Frank said. He turned to Oscar who had paled visibly. "We'll want high powered rifles with needle nose bullets."

CRAB POINT was a long finger of mainland reaching toward the boat on the port side. Already the ocean swell was taking a firm grip on the boat's motion, giving it a fore and aft rhythm that under ordinary circumstances would have been soothing. Far ahead a blue mist obscured the horizon. To the stern the town lay along the curving shore in picturesque panorama.

Oscar Freeman, the police chief, glanced sternward at Jack Sprout who was standing at the tiller, running his fingers over the spokes of the wheel lovingly. Oscar's eyes softened. He knew how much Jack loved his boat, the only thing he owned.

His gaze shifted around to the three policemen standing up in the fish hold, rifles ready, nervous tenseness visible in their every line.

He frowned at the narrow door to the cabin. Behind that locked door Helen was being too quiet. It made Oscar uneasy to have her so quiet.

He went over and bent down to look through one of the windows. Helen was sitting on a bunk, her back straight, her face relaxed, her eyes staring into space.

He went back to where the two doctors were standing.

"She's just sitting there," he growled.

Crab Point slipped to the sternward. There was no sound except the slapping of the salt water against the hull and the muted powerful sound of the motor under the deck where they stood.

"What made you believe Jack's story?" Dr. Nelson asked suddenly. "I saw so much evidence of Freudian symbolism cropping out that I was sure it was a fabrication of the mind."

"And you were right," Frank said quietly. "Most of it was a fabrication of the mind. I saw that evidence myself. There were one or two things that couldn't possibly be that, however."

He took out a cigarette and lit it, cupping his lighter in his hands.

"Did it ever occur to you," he went on, "that ocean or lake water contains enough oxygen so that if a human being could breathe it like air is breathed it would be possible to live underwater? A fish out of water can live a long time by getting its oxygen from the air, provided its gills are kept moist. In the same way people could breathe water if they could get it into their lungs. It's a well known fact that death by drowning is a sort of strangulation. Very little water gets into the lungs. The reason for that is that the phlegm in the throat and the bronchial tract gells and prevents the water from entering. Panic adds to the complications.

"If that panic could be avoided and a person was to breathe through the mouth, it might be possible to switch from air breathing to water breathing." Frank smiled at the amazed expressions on Oscar's and Dr. Nelson's faces. "Under hypnotism it would be possible not only to prevent the panic but to convince the subject that such a thing was natural. Especially if the hypnotist were *a water breather by nature.*

"I'd never heard of it being done before, but when Jack Sprout described how Frieda climbed aboard and bent over, forcing the water from her lungs so she could breathe air again, I knew that he was describing something that actually happened. It was a thing utterly beyond his ability to imagine either consciously or subconsciously."

"I can see that now," Dr. Nelson said. "But even if I'd seen it at once I would have dismissed it. The implications are even more incredible than it would have been to admit the possibility of him being able to imagine it."

"There was something else though," Frank said. "It was his sudden feeling that something was radically different about Frieda when he took her in his arms and kissed her. So different that even though he was in the throws of physical passion and he held an undressed and very beautiful girl in his arms he suddenly thrust her away and headed back for shore to escape. Why? He hadn't felt that way the instant before... The symbolism would be obvious, if it were a symbolism. Then it could be said that in reality it had been the other way around. She had repulsed him, and after he killed her it twisted to him repulsing her. But there was a more natural explanation. If she were in a hypnotic trance at the time it would explain his reaction.

"Then there were her clothes on the beach at Crab Point. They could have been planted there, but it was more consistent with the overall picture if she had gone out there deliberately and swam out to sea. *To join the being that lurked out there, calling to her.*" He turned bleak eyes to the calm surface of the water gliding past. Oscar and Dr. Nelson followed his gaze, sensing the horror that lurked under that calm screen, "A being, perhaps out of the unexplored depths of the mid-Atlantic. A being who has come close to shore and is using its powers to call its prey to it, even from dry land, just as a certain kind of snake can hypnotize its prey, and who lurks out there even now, calling to Helen as it called to Frieda." He sighed deeply. "You see, Helen is a very gifted psychic and has been under hypnosis so many times she's extremely sensitive to it. It was Frieda Thorne's sensitiveness that made her the first victim."

"And the last, I hope," Oscar said grimly.

THE BOAT pitched suddenly to the starboard. The surface of the water boiled darkly. A shot punctuated the atmosphere.

"Stop that!" Frank said. "I told you not to fire until you could actually see something."

"Sorry, sir," the policeman who had fired said sheepishly.

Frank surveyed the unnaturally white faces of the men, the grim lines of his face relaxing slightly. "We've got to be cool," he said. "This thing, whatever it is, is big enough to rock a twenty foot boat."

"I thought Jack said it was a giant flounder," Oscar said.

Frank shook his head. "I think it can look different to different people. In other words, the shape you will see will be what your mind paints. Not its actual shape."

He went to the cabin and stooped to look in a window. Helen had taken off her clothes. She was standing in the center of the cabin, her head cocked to one side as though she were listening to some distant voice. As he watched she went to the door.

"Be ready with your rifles," he warned.

He went to the door and unlocked it.

"Shut off your motor and drift," he said to Jack Sprout. Then to Oscar, "It may take the two of us to hold her if she tries to jump overboard."

The cabin door opened slowly. There was a universal gasp as Helen emerged slowly to stand on the deck.

Apparently unconscious of her nakedness she turned her head this way and that, sniffing the air delicately, a dreamy smile on her lips. Her eyes fell on Oscar.

"Oh, hello, darling," she said casually. "Isn't it nice weather? I think I'll go in for a swim. You don't mind do you?"

Her expression was one of utter innocence.

Oscar darted a questioning glance at Frank, who nodded.

"Of course I don't mind, Helen," Oscar said.

"You're a dear," Helen said. She stepped up to him and put her arms over his shoulders; her breasts lightly touching his shirt front.

He stood frozen, an expression of torture on his face.

Helen began to breathe deeply. Her eyes widened, glowing with inner excitement.

"Don't let her go, Oscar!" Frank said sharply.

The ship was rocking noticeably now from the motion of something under the surface. An electrical tension seemed to be building up in the atmosphere around the ship.

Helen started to step back from Oscar. Quickly he circled her waist with his arms.

"Let me go, Oscar," Helen said cajolingly. "I just want to take a short dip." Her voice sharpened angrily. "Let me go!"

The boat was rocking more violently now. It tipped suddenly to one side. Oscar fell, dragging Helen with him.

There was a flash of white as she broke free of his embrace and darted to the edge of the deck. She poised there an instant while Frank and Dr. Nelson leaped toward her. Then she was a white arc cutting into the water.

"Cover us!" Oscar shouted. He had gotten to his feet. He dived in where Helen had disappeared.

Helen had surfaced. Oscar's head appeared a few feet from hers. He was trying to get to her, his clothing hampering him.

The three police were methodically spacing their rifle fire around them.

Suddenly the motor roared into life. The boat picked up speed, making a wide circle around the two figures in the water. A pile of neatly folded net at the stern was being pulled into the water to form a circling arc of floats bobbing in the water. The boat completed its circle. Jack Sprout was in his element now, doing his work with the skill and instinct inherited from generations of fishermen.

Something appeared just under the surface. The rifle shots switched to it, but it had dropped out of sight. Jack had stopped the motor after reversing it and halting the boat. Now he began hauling in the net.

Oscar had reached Helen and was struggling with her to keep her from diving under. The net settled against them, holding them.

The scaled back of a giant fish broke the surface just outside the net. Instantly the three rifles spat. Again, and again. Suddenly the finned back dissolved into nothing.

At the same instant Helen grew slack in Oscar's arms. Jack drew in the net until Frank and Dr. Nelson could reach down and take Helen's hands and draw her up.

JACK SPROUT went into the cabin and brought out a long poled gaff. He reached down into the widening pool of dark red and hooked it into the bulbous mass floating there. The hook took hold for a moment, then pulled through.

Helen, a robe drawn around her, stood within the encirclement of Oscar Freeman's arm, a dazed expression on her face. The others were watching the thing with a mixture of repugnance and fascination on their faces.

"It won't hook," Jack said. "Some kind of pulpy stuff that falls apart. What's that red stuff in the water? Blood?"

Something white appeared under the surface. With a grunt Jack hooked it, drawing it to the surface.

For a brief instant an almost human face was there, deeply sunken eyes of coal black glaring at them. There were black holes in the oily smooth skull shape—bullet punctures.

Then the thing parted as the gaff went through it as though it were rotten flesh. It paused just below the red surface of the water. A large bubble of air broke the surface. The whole shapeless mass slowly dropped out of sight until there was nothing but the red stain, slowly floating away.

With a hurt cry Helen turned to huddle against Oscar. He pulled her close against him, comforting her.

"What a horrible creature," Dr. Nelson whispered hoarsely.

"It's probably best that it wouldn't hold together so we could take it to shore," Frank said. "I only hope there are no more of its kind. Vampires of the deep."

"That thing looked almost human. Its face, anyway," Jack Sprout said.

"Perhaps it was, Jack," Frank said. "Yes, I rather think that once, long ago, it was—human."

Helen crept closer into Oscar's arms, sobbing softly.

THE END

THE GOLGOTHA DANCERS

By Manly Wade Wellman

A curious and terrifying story about an artist who sold his soul that he might paint a living picture.

I had come to the Art Museum to see the special show of Goya prints, but that particular gallery was so crowded that I could hardly get in, much less see or savor anything; wherefore I walked out again. I wandered through the other wings with their rows and rows of oils, their Greek and Roman sculptures, their stern ranks of medieval armors, their Oriental porcelains, their Egyptian gods. At length, by chance and not by design, I came to the head of a certain rear stairway. Other habitués of the museum will know the one I mean when I remind them that Arnold Böcklin's *The Isle of the Dead* hangs on the wall of the landing.

I started down, relishing in advance the impression Böcklin's picture would make with its high brown rocks and black poplars, its midnight sky and gloomy film of sea, its single white figure erect in the bow of the beach-nosing skiff. But, as I descended, I saw that *The Isle of the Dead* was not in its accustomed position on the wall. In that space, arresting even in the bad light and from the up-angle of the stairs, hung a gilt-framed painting I had never seen or heard of in all my museum-haunting years.

I gazed at it, one will imagine, all the way down to the landing. Then I had a close, searching look, and a final appraising stare from the lip of the landing above the lower half of the flight. So far as I can learn—and I have been diligent in my research—the thing is unknown even to the best-informed of art experts. Perhaps it is as well that I describe it in detail.

It seemed to represent action upon a small plateau or table rock, drab and bare, with a twilight sky deepening into a starless evening. This setting, restrainedly worked up in blue-grays and blue-blacks, was not the first thing to catch the eye, however. The front of the picture was filled with lively dancing creatures, as pink, plump and naked as cherubs and as patently evil as the meditations of Satan in his rare idle moments.

I counted those dancers. There were twelve of them, ranged in a half-circle, and they were cavorting in evident glee around a central object—a prone cross, which appeared to be made of two stout logs with some of the bark still upon them. To this cross a pair of the pink things—that makes fourteen—kneeling and swinging blocky-looking hammers or mauls, spiked a human figure.

I say *human* when I speak of that figure, and I withhold the word in describing the dancers and their hammer-wielding fellows. There is a reason. The supine victim on the cross was a beautifully represented male body, as clear and anatomically correct as an illustration in a surgical textbook. The head was writhed around, as if in pain, and I could not see the face or its expression; but in the tortured tenseness of the muscles, in the slaty white sheen of the skin with jagged streaks of vivid gore upon it, agonized nature was plain and doubly plain. I could almost see the painted limbs writhe against the transfixing nails.

By the same token, the dancers and hammerers were so dynamically done as to seem half in motion before my eyes. So much for the sound skill of the painter. Yet, where the crucified prisoner was all clarity, these others were all fog. No lines, no angles, no muscles—their features could not be seen or sensed. I was not even sure if they had hair or not. It was as if each was picked out with a ray of light in that surrounding dusk, light that revealed and yet shimmered indistinctly; light, too, that had absolutely nothing of comfort or honesty in it.

"Hold on, there!" came a sharp challenge from the stairs behind and below me. "What are you doing? And what's that picture doing?"

I started so that I almost lost my footing and fell upon the speaker—one of the Museum guards. He was a slight old fellow and his thin hair was gray, but he advanced upon me with all the righteous, angry pluck of a beefy policeman. His attitude surprised and nettled me.

"I was going to ask somebody that same question," I told him as austerely as I could manage. "What about this picture? I thought there was a Böcklin hanging here."

The guard relaxed his forbidding attitude at first sound of my voice. "Oh, I beg your pardon, sir. I thought you were somebody else—the man who brought that thing." He nodded at the picture, and the hostile glare came back into his eyes. "It so happened that he talked to me first, then to the curator. Said it was art—great art—and the Museum must have it." He lifted his shoulders, in a shrug or a shudder. "Personally, I think it's plain beastly."

So it was, I grew aware as I looked at it again. "And the Museum has accepted it at last?" I prompted.

He shook his head. "Oh, no, sir. An hour ago he was at the back door, with that nasty daub there under his arm. I heard part of the argument. He got insulting, and he was told to clear out and take his picture with him. But he must have got in here somehow, and hung it himself." Walking close to the painting, as gingerly as though he expected the pink dancers to leap out at him, he pointed to the lower edge of the frame. "If it was a real Museum piece, we'd have a plate right there, with the name of the painter and the title."

I, too, came close. There was no plate, just as the guard had said. But in the lower left-hand corner of the canvas were sprawling capitals, pale paint on the dark, spelling out the word *GOLGOTHA*. Beneath these, in small, barely readable script:

I sold my soul that I might paint a living picture.

No signature or other clue to the artist's identity.

The guard had discovered a great framed rectangle against the wall to one side. "Here's the picture he took down," he informed me, highly relieved. "Help me put it back, will you, sir? And do you suppose," here he grew almost wistful, "that we could get rid of this other thing before someone finds I let the crazy fool slip past me?"

I took one edge of *The Isle of the Dead* and lifted it to help him hang it once more.

"Tell you what," I offered on sudden impulse; "I'll take this *Golgotha* piece home with me, if you like."

"Would you do that?" he almost yelled out in his joy at the suggestion. "Would you, to oblige me?"

"To oblige myself," I returned. "I need another picture at my place."

And the upshot of it was, he smuggled me and the unwanted painting out of the Museum. Never mind how. I have done quite enough as it is to jeopardize his job and my own welcome up there.

It was not until I had paid off my taxi and lugged the unwieldy parallelogram of canvas and wood upstairs to my bachelor apartment that I bothered to wonder if it might be valuable. I never did find out, but from the first I was deeply impressed.

Hung over my own fireplace, it looked as large and living as a scene glimpsed through a window or, perhaps, on a stage in a theater. The capering pink bodies caught new lights from my lamp, lights that glossed and intensified their shape and color but did not reveal any new details. I pored once more over the cryptic legend: *I sold my soul that I might paint a living picture.*

A living picture—was it that? I could not answer. For all my honest delight in such things, I cannot be called expert or even knowing as regards art. Did I even like the Golgotha painting? I could not be sure of that, either. And the rest of the inscription, about selling a soul; I was considerably intrigued by that, and let my thoughts ramble on the subject of Satanist complexes and the vagaries of half-crazy painters. As I read, that evening, I glanced up again and again at my new possession. Sometimes it seemed ridiculous, sometimes sinister. Shortly after midnight I rose, gazed once more, and then turned out the parlor lamp. For a moment, or so it seemed, I could see those dancers, so many dim-pink silhouettes in the sudden darkness. I went to the kitchen for a bit of whisky and water, and thence to my bedroom.

I had dreams. In them I was a boy again, and my mother and sister were leaving the house to go to a theater where— think of it!—Richard Mansfield would play *Beau Brummell.* I, the youngest, was told to stay at home and mind the troublesome furnace. I wept copiously in my disappointed loneliness, and then Mansfield himself stalked in, in full Brummell regalia. He laughed goldenly and stretched out his hand in warm greeting. I, the lad of my dreams, put out my own hand, then was frightened when he would not loosen his grasp. I tugged, and he laughed again. The gold of his laughter turned suddenly hard, cold. I tugged with all my strength, and woke.

Something held me tight by the wrist.

In my first half-moment of wakefulness I was aware that the room was filled with the pink dancers of the picture, in nimble, fierce-happy motion. They were man-size, too, or nearly so, visible in the dark with the dim radiance of fox-fire. On the small scale of the painting they had seemed no more than babyishly plump; now they were gross, like huge erect toads. And, as I awakened fully, they were closing in, a menacing ring of them, around my bed. One stood at my right side, and its grip, clumsy and rubbery-hard like that of a monkey, was closed upon my arm.

I saw and sensed all this, as I say, in a single moment. With the sensing came the realization of peril, so great that I did not stop to wonder at the uncanniness of my visitors. I tried frantically to jerk loose. For the moment I did not succeed and as I thrashed about, throwing my body nearly across the bed, a second dancer dashed in from the left. It seized and clamped my other arm. I felt, rather than heard, a wave of soft, wordless merriment from them all. My heart and sinews seemed to fail, and briefly I lay still in a daze of horror, pinned down crucifix-fashion between my two captors.

Was that a *hammer* raised above me as I sprawled?

There rushed and swelled into me the sudden startled strength that sometimes favors the desperate. I screamed like any wild thing caught in a trap, rolled somehow out of bed and to my feet. One of the beings I shook off and the other I dashed against the bureau. Freed, I made for the bedroom door and the front of the apartment, stumbling and staggering on fear-weakened legs.

One of the dim-shining pink things barred my way at the very threshold, and the others were closing in behind, as if for a sudden rush. I flung my right fist with all my strength and weight. The being bobbed back unresistingly before my smash, like a rubber toy floating through water. I plunged past, reached the entry and fumbled for the knob of the outer door.

They were all about me then, their rubbery palms fumbling at my shoulders, my elbows, my pajama jacket. They would have dragged me down before I could negotiate the lock. A racking shudder possessed me and seemed to flick them clear. Then I stumbled against a stand, and purely by good luck my hand fell upon a bamboo walking-stick. I yelled again, in truly hysterical fierceness, and laid about me as with a whip. My blows did little or no damage to those unearthly assailants, but they shrank back, teetering and dancing, to a safe distance. Again I had the sense that they were laughing, mocking. For the moment I had beaten them off, but they were sure of me in the end. Just then my groping free hand pressed a switch. The entry sprang into light.

On the instant they were not there.

Somebody was knocking outside, and with trembling fingers I turned the knob of the door. In came a tall, slender girl with a blue lounging-robe caught hurriedly around her. Her bright hair was disordered as though she had just sprung from her bed.

"Is someone sick?" she asked in a breathless voice. "I live down the hall—I heard cries." Her round blue eyes were studying my face, which must have been ghastly pale. "You see, I'm a trained nurse, and perhaps———"

"Thank God you did come!" I broke in, unceremoniously but honestly, and went before her to turn on every lamp in the parlor.

It was she who, without guidance, searched out my whisky and siphon and mixed for me a highball of grateful strength. My teeth rang nervously on the edge of the glass as I gulped it down. After that I got my own robe—a becoming one, with satin facings—and sat with her on the divan to tell of my adventure. When I had finished, she gazed long at the painting of the dancers, then back at me. Her eyes, like two chips of the April sky, were full of concern and she held her rosy lower lip between her teeth. I thought that she was wonderfully pretty.

"What a perfectly terrible nightmare," she said.

"It was no nightmare," I protested.

She smiled and argued the point, telling me all manner of comforting things about mental associations and their reflections in vivid dreams.

To clinch her point she turned to the painting.

"This line about a 'living picture' is the peg on which your slumbering mind hung the whole fabric," she suggested, her slender fingertip touching the painted scribble. "Your very literal subconscious self didn't understand that the artist meant his picture would live only figuratively."

"Are you sure that's what the artist meant?" I asked, but finally I let her convince me. One can imagine how badly I wanted to be convinced.

She mixed me another highball, and a short one for herself. Over it she told me her name—Miss Dolby—and finally she left me with a last comforting assurance. But, nightmare or no, I did not sleep again that night. I sat in the parlor among the lamps, smoking and dipping into book after book. Countless times I felt my gaze drawn back to the painting over the fireplace, with the cross and the nail-pierced wretch and the shimmering pink dancers.

After the rising sun had filled the apartment with its honest light and cheer I felt considerably calmer. I slept all morning, and in the afternoon was disposed to agree with Miss Dolby that the whole business had been a bad dream, nothing more. Dressing, I went down the hall, knocked on her door and invited her to dinner with me.

It was a good dinner. Afterward we went to an amusing motion picture, with Charles Butterworth in it as I remember. After bidding her goodnight, I went to my own place. Undressed and in bed, I lay awake. My late morning slumber made my eyes slow to close. Thus it was that I heard the faint shuffle of feet and, sitting up against my pillows, saw the glowing silhouettes of the Golgotha dancers. Alive and magnified, they were creeping into my bedroom.

I did not hesitate or shrink this time. I sprang up, tense and defiant.

"No, you don't!" I yelled at them. As they seemed to hesitate before the impact of my wild voice, I charged frantically. For a moment I scattered them and got through the bedroom door, as on the previous night. There was another shindy in the entry; this time they all got hold of me, like a pack of hounds, and wrestled me back against the wall. I writhe even now when I think of the unearthly hardness of their little gripping paws. Two on each arm were spread-eagling me upon the plaster. The cruciform position again!

I swore, yelled and kicked. One of them was in the way of my foot. He floated back, unhurt. That was their strength and horror—their ability to go flabby and non-resistant under smashing, flattening blows. Something tickled my palm, pricked it. The point of a spike...

"Miss Dolby!" I shrieked, as a child might call for its mother. "Help! Miss D——"

The door flew open; I must not have locked it. "Here I am," came her unafraid reply.

She was outlined against the rectangle of light from the hall. My assailants let go of me to dance toward her. She gasped but did not scream. I staggered along the wall, touched a light-switch, and the parlor just beyond us flared into visibility. Miss Dolby and I ran in to the lamp, rallying there as stone-age folk must have rallied at their fire to face the monsters of the night. I looked at her; she was still fully dressed, as I had left her, apparently she had been sitting up. Her rouge made flat patches on her pale cheeks, but her eyes were level.

This time the dancers did not retreat or vanish; they lurked in the comparative gloom of the entry, jigging and trembling as if mustering their powers and resolutions for another rush at us.

"You see," I chattered out to her, "it wasn't a nightmare."

She spoke, not in reply, but as if to herself. "They have no faces," she whispered. "*No faces!*" In the half-light that was diffused upon them from our lamp they presented the featurelessness of so many huge gingerbread boys, covered with pink icing. One of them, some kind of leader, pressed forward within the circle of the light. It daunted him a bit. He hesitated, but did not retreat.

From my center table Miss Dolby had picked up a bright paper-cutter. She poised it with the assurance of one who knows how to handle cutting instruments.

"When they come," she said steadily, "let's stand close together. We'll be harder to drag down that way."

I wanted to shout my admiration of her fearless front toward the dreadful beings, my thankfulness for her quick run to my rescue. All I could mumble was, "You're mighty brave."

She turned for a moment to look at the picture above my dying fire. My eyes followed hers. I think I expected to see a blank canvas—find that the painted dancers had vanished from it and had grown into the living ones. But they were still in the picture, and the cross and the victim were there, too. Miss Dolby read aloud the inscription:

"*A living picture…* The artist knew what he was talking about, after all."

"Couldn't a living picture be killed?" I wondered.

It sounded uncertain, and a childish quibble to boot, but Miss Dolby exclaimed triumphantly, as at an inspiration.

"Killed? Yes!" she shouted. She sprang at the picture, darting out with the paper-cutter. The point ripped into one of the central figures in the dancing semicircle.

All the crowd in the entry seemed to give a concerted throb, as of startled protest. I swung, heart racing, to front them again. What had happened? Something had changed, I saw. The intrepid leader had vanished. No, he had not drawn back into the group. He had vanished.

Miss Dolby, too, had seen. She struck again, gashed the painted representation of another dancer. And this time the vanishing happened before my eyes, a creature at the rear of the group went out of existence as suddenly and completely as though a light had blinked out.

The others, driven by their danger, rushed.

I met them, feet planted. I tried to embrace them all at once, went over backward under them. I struck, wrenched, tore. I think I even bit something grisly and bloodless, like fungoid tissue, but I refuse to remember for certain. One or two of the forms struggled past me and grappled Miss Dolby. I struggled to my feet and pulled them back from her. There were not so many swarming after me now. I fought hard before they got me down again. And Miss Dolby kept tearing and stabbing at the canvas—again, again. Clutches melted from my throat, my arms. There were only two dancers left. I flung them back and rose. Only one left. Then none.

They were gone, gone into nowhere.

"That did it," said Miss Dolby breathlessly.

She had pulled the picture down. It was only a frame now, with ragged ribbons of canvas dangling from it.

I snatched it out of her hands and threw it upon the coals of the fire.

"Look," I urged her joyfully. "It's burning! That's the end. Do you see?"

"Yes, I see," she answered slowly. "Some fiend-ridden artist—his evil genius brought it to life."

"The inscription is the literal truth, then?" I supplied.

"Truth no more." She bent to watch the burning. "As the painted figures were destroyed, their incarnations faded."

We said nothing further, but sat down together and gazed as the flames ate the last thread of fabric, the last splinter of wood. Finally we looked up again and smiled at each other.

All at once I knew that I loved her.

THE END

SOMETHING OLD

By Mary Elizabeth Counselman

Thoughts are things… as the saying goes.

IT WAS a home wedding. Perhaps if it had been held in a church, even in the pastor's chapel, the whole hideous thing would not have happened. In the holy atmosphere of a church, standing before an actual altar, when Celia Mitchell said: *"I do!"* she would have been safe from the evil Force that…

But it was a home wedding. In the Mitchells' big living room, cleared of furniture now except for folding chairs borrowed from the city auditorium, flowers were banked along the walls. Guests were seated already, facing the picture window against which the pastor would stand to perform the ceremony. They kept up a low murmur of conversation, which died down only when Mary McPherson, near the piano, began to sing *"O Promise Me"* in her low sweet contralto.

In the library Bob Hanson, the young assistant curator of the museum, was standing first on one foot, then on the other. He grinned feebly at his white-haired "best man," who was also his superior and his uncle, Walter Ferris grinned back at him, patting his vest pocket.

"Yes, yes, I've got the ring!" he chuckled. "It's right here. In fact," he added humorously, "I happen to have six *more rings* on my person—if the one you bought for Celia gets lost!" At his nephew's puzzled look, the curator pulled out a small leather case and flipped it open, revealing half a dozen curious-looking circles of metal and semi-precious mineral. "Ran into Peabody on my way over here," he explained, and he handed me the shipment from London. Nice specimens, aren't they?"

The bridegroom nodded absently, tugging at his collar. For perhaps the tenth time in the past three minutes, he glanced at his watch, muttering something about medieval torture as a way to start two people off on a happy marriage. Then he started nervously, as the study door flung open and a little girl in a frilly white dress dashed in, swinging her basket of rose petals. She beamed at her brother-in-law to-be and caught at his hand affectionately, displaying a missing front tooth in a smile.

"Bob! Thelia thaid would you or Misther Ferrith let her have thomething out of the mutheum? Anything little, for her to wear or hold. Mary lent her a garter to wear for *'borrowed,'* and she'th got thomething *'new'* and *'blue'* on her underclothes. But not anything *'old'*...!" the child, a sevenyear-old edition of her sister, brought out the words in a breathless rush. "Thelia won't thtart without it! Mama thays it'th bad luck!"

Both men laughed, grateful for any diversion to ease the tension of waiting. Ferris, amused, reached for the phone, then suddenly remembered the leather case he had thrust back into his pocket. Snapping it open again, still laughing, he regarded the rings for a moment—a Fifth Century Syrian ring of banded agate, an Irish one of twisted wire, a leather English band cut from the finger of a glove, an East Indian thumb-ring of iron and silver. The white-haired curator of the museum peered at the collection briefly, then selected one of heavy black metal, hexagonal in shape, on each face of which was inscribed a queer symbol. He handed this to the little flower girl with an exaggerated bow.

"Here you are, my dear! This is probably the oldest relic in our collection—an old Babylonian betrothal ring, from the looks of it. You may tell the fair bride," he added with a twinkle in his faded blue eyes, "that the inscription reads...oh, something like: *'Mine, beloved; mine through eternity.'* Very romantic, eh?" He winked at the child, adding gallantly, "Don't tell your sister *I* sent it. Tell her it was Bob! Hmm?"

The little flower girl nodded, with the sly giggle of a conspirator in romance. She disappeared through the study doorway again—and in a moment, the first strains of *Lohengrin* seeped into the quiet room. Bob straightened like a doomed man marching to the Chair, then laughed at his uncle sheepishly.

"The things we helpless men go through," he complained as they walked out together to stand beside the altar. There already, the fat pastor was beaming beneficently out over the throng, waiting for the bride to come pacing slowly down the aisle on her father's arm.

THEN she appeared, a pale blond vision in white satin with a chaplet of orange blossoms around the crown of her veil. If there had been a small white silk-covered Bible in her hands, instead of a bouquet of orchids and lilies-of-the-valley... But it was a bouquet Celia carried, smiling tremulously at her baby sister, dancing ahead of her to scatter rose petals. On her right hand—the only ring she wore—Bob noticed the heavy antique circlet. He grinned, casting a grateful glance at his uncle. The old rascal: wouldn't give him a raise in salary large enough to cover a diamond, along with the lovely little cottage Bob had built for Celia. But at the last minute, he *would* make a gesture like this—giving his nephew's bride an ancient betrothal ring that must have cost the museum a sum well into five figures. Old Walter Ferris, his nephew suspected fondly, was constantly at war within himself between what he wanted to be, a hard-boiled executive, and what he was, a sentimental dreamer.

At that moment Celia stepped to a place beside him, and the young assistant curator could see nothing else beyond her lovely excited face.

"Dearly beloved," intoned the pastor, "we are gathered here together in the sight of God to unite this man and this woman in..."

Bob sighed, slipping a loving little wink at the girl by his side. Then, abruptly, his eyes went grave and anxious, observing on the face of his bride a sudden startled expression. She was not looking at him, but beyond him, beyond his uncle also, at a shadowy spot beyond the altar. Her slim white throat contracted all at once, as though she were fighting hard to stifle a scream that welled up from her inmost being. Bob followed her gaze, but could see nothing. Then he noticed that Celia was tugging at the heavy ring on her finger, trying to get it off. This in itself was puzzling, as the thing had seemed at least two sizes too large for her slender hand. Now, though, it would not come off, not even turn. As she twisted at it frantically, a tiny drop of blood welled out from under the broad dark metal and splashed redly upon her white satin skirt.

"Do you, Robert Edward Hanson, take this woman to be...?" the pastor was asking in a ringing voice.

Bob replied in an absent murmur, staring at his bride's hand. Celia glanced at him with a helpless little grimace, and whispered:

"Darling, the ring—it won't come off! What'll I do? It's so *tight* all at once..."

Her husband-to-be moved closer to her, with a protective gesture that caused watching matrons to breathe a fluttery sigh of reminiscence.

"Don't worry about it, sweetheart," Bob whispered back, smiling. "We'll have it filed off later. Does it hurt you?"

"Yes!" Celia whispered. "It... My finger must be swelling. It's cutting me terribly!"

"Do you, Celia Anne Mitchell, take this man...?" the pastor pursued, frowning sternly at, this whispered interruption.

"I do!" the bride pronounced—followed by a little gasp, quickly suppressed. Again Bob, and his uncle as well, saw her tug at the ring, as a second, then a third drop of blood ooze from beneath it to splash over the virgin whiteness of her wedding dress.

Then in a swift rush of words and ritual, the ceremony was over, and the young couple was climbing into Bob's waiting car, laughing and dodging the rain of rice that was thrown at them. Celia, in a pale blue suit and straw hat with tiny pink flowers under the brim, nestled close to her new husband as they drove away, followed by a clanking tail of tin cans and old shoes tied to the rear bumper.

"Thank heavens that's over!" the girl laughed, breathlessly. "Now you're supposed to put your arm around me and say, 'Alone, at last!' That's part of the ceremony!

Bob obeyed, reciting "Alone-at-last" with such mechanical lack of expression that Celia pinched his arm.

"My cavalier!" she peered, then her expression softened as she glanced down at the massive ring on her right hand, looking awkward and ill-fashioned in contrast to the slim platinum band on her left hand. "But you *are* romantic, after all," she sighed. "Oh, Bob, it was such a dear thing to do—giving me this old, old ring from a collection. A Babylonian betrothal ring, your uncle said. And the inscription is just perfect!"

Her husband gulped guiltily, then decided that this was one of the few things he would not tell her. Instead, he patted her hand.

"I picked it out just for you," he lied happily. "You wouldn't let me spend our refrigerator fund on a solitaire, remember! Frugal little housewife already, aren't you?" he teased, then frowned. "But I was worried at the ceremony. About that ring, I mean." He poked at the dark band, which now hung loosely on the girl's finger. "Wonder why your knuckle swelled up like that? Some sort of allergy to the metal, do you suppose?"

THE bride shrugged, slipping off her hat and nestling her head on his shoulder. "Oh—nerves, probably. But it...it seemed all at once to have *tightened*. And...then..." She stopped, laughing and shrugging. "Oh, for goodness sake. I haven't seen a bogeyman in a dark corner since I was Betsy's age! And didn't she look darling?" Celia prattled on happily. "Bob... Let's not wait too long to start having children of our own. First, I'd like to have a—"

"Bogeyman?" Bob interrupted, amused. "What did you mean by—?"

"Oh—nerves again!" The girl tossed off his solicitude. "It was when the minister started— And then again, just as I said: *'I do!'* Over there in that shadowy corner beyond the piano.

I...I thought I saw something, that's all." She laughed lightly, but the man noticed a small shiver ripple down her bare arms, in a wake of gooseflesh that felt rough to his caressive touch.

"Saw what? The ghost of your wicked past?" he jibed pleasantly. "All those poor broken-hearted guys who promptly jumped off ninety-nine bridges when they read our wedding announcement in the paper?"

Celia made a face at him, then dropped her eyes uncertainly. Once again that odd little shiver swept over her like a breath of cold wind.

"No; it was—well, at first it looked like a dog! A huge shaggy wet dog, like a Saint Bernard. And—dark gray all over, except that the *head*—" She shuddered now visibly, pressing closer to the man at the wheel and pulling his arm around her shoulders. "Oh, let's not talk about it any more!" she begged. "It was just a silly fancy! Here, darling, keep this for me. It's so heavy, and it keeps slipping off. I wouldn't ever, ever want to lose it! *'Mine, beloved; mine through eternity!'"* she quoted the inscription softly, then slipped the big ring into Bob's pocket.

THE small mountain hotel they had chosen for their honeymoon was perched on a laurel-crested ridge overlooking five states. As they entered the lobby self-consciously and approached the desk, a benign little man popped up from nowhere, snapping his fingers at a sleepy-eyed Negro porter.

"Bridal suite?" he whispered, winking at Bob in a way that sent a titter over those wandering about in the lobby. "Oh, the Hansons—of course! Have your reservation right here. Yes, yes," he added archly, still in that stage whisper that left the young couple flushed and giggling. "Honeymooners? You'll be happy to know that our bridal suite is soundproofed! Nobody listening in to those sweet nothings you'll want to say to this charming young lady!"

Closing the door after the grinning porter a few minutes later, Bob and Celia burst out laughing, and melted together in a long kiss. Arms entwined, they stood for a moment, looking out through a broad French door that opened upon a small balcony. Below it, the mountain fell away in a green sweep of treetops, completing the illusion that they were alone on some tiny planet suspended far above the earth. The girl sighed.

"Oh, Bob, I'm so glad we could get the bridal suite! Mother and Dad spent their honeymoon here, I think I told you. And…and that's why I wanted so much to…" She broke off shyly, glancing at him from the corner of her eye. "Darling?" she whispered. "Let me have my ring back—I want to wear it while—while you run down and get me a pack of cigarettes, or something. Would you? That's part of the ceremony, too! Then we'll have dinner sent up to us, and watch the sun go down. Oh, Bob, I love you so much!" She flung herself into his arms happily, then shoved him toward the door, laughing.

Bob handed her the ring, and went out, smiling softly to himself.

Because of his solicitude for his bride, for her shy feeling of strangeness, he wandered about the lobby below for perhaps half an hour.

(Perhaps if he had not done so— But there are so many ifs, as Walter Ferris remarked to me later, when he told me the strange story.)

Actually it had begun at the ceremony. But, to Bob, knocking on the locked door of his bridal suite, it began just there—

For, Celia, his bride, would not open the door. Dusk had fallen over the mountains outside, and a few faint stars were already creeping into the sky. Bob knocked again, more loudly, calling his wife's name. There was an answer—a harsh shrill voice, shouting at him in a language he had never heard before. A woman's voice. It sounded, he said, like Celia's and yet not like her soft mellow tones. He was able to distinguish one or two words *"ziggurat,"* and *"shimtu,"* then a string of words that sounded peculiarly like a chant: *"inuma iluawelum…"*

At that, startled and anxious, he began to hammer on the door, aware of other sounds that issued through the locked portal. There was, as he described it, a *rushing* sound, as of a high wind blowing—although the night outside was still and warm, with heat lightning flickering across the southern sky. Twice he heard what he described as a deep, horrible growling noise, like an ape, but with a queer suggestion of words.

Then, frantic, he began to batter the door down by charging against it with his broad young shoulder. It splintered at the third impact, and the young bridegroom almost fell inside, followed closely by the porter and the benign-faced clerk who had heard the commotion from below.

Celia lay on the broad bed, clad in a pale green negligee that hung in ribbons, all but torn from her body. Blood ran from her bruised mouth, and there was hardly a spot on her slender half-nude body that did not bear some mark of violence. She lay face up, moaning, her eyes half closed. But as all three men noted as they ran to her side, her expression was not one of horror or pain, but of ineffable *ecstasy;* of a wild, almost hysterical *happiness!* Her bruised lips moved once, uttering a single syllable, as Bob bent over her, his young face contorted with distress.

"Bell—?" he repeated. "What bell, darling? Oh, couldn't you ring for help? Who was it? How the devil did that...that fiend get in, whoever it was that..." He whirled on the frightened desk clerk, then glared beyond them at the cluster of guests who hovered in the doorway. *"Do something,"* Bob grated. "Call the police! My...my wife has been..." He left the ugly words mercifully unspoken, then turned to press Celia's hand to his cheek, cursing and crooning to her.

As he did so, the massive Babylonian ring slipped from her finger and rolled at his feet. A section of the hexagonal outer part fell open, and the young husband picked it up distractedly, staring at the concealed compartment. Inside, framed in a thin gold triangle, was a tiny piece of fabric that at first seemed to be silk, yellow silk, interwoven with a coarse dark thread.

Then Bob glanced up as the hotel doctor shoved his way into the room, firmly closing the door after him. Ordering all but the distraught bridegroom out into the hall, he bent over the half-conscious girl, who was now beginning to moan and toss in pain. His face was bleak as he turned on Bob, lips compressed.

"You did this?" he snapped coldly, "Young man, I certainly recommend psychiatric treatment—and an immediate annulment of your marriage!—if you... Veteran, are you? Sometimes, in delayed cases of combat fatigue—"

"Oh, stop it!" Bob ground out through his teeth. "I was down in the lobby! Somebody must have knocked after I left. And Celia opened the door, thinking it was I. It's a cinch nobody could have got in by way of the balcony!

THE medico stared at him, bewildered but unconvinced. He shook his graying head, shrugged helplessly, and tried to calm this pleasant-looking young man—who might or might not be a violent lunatic.

"All right, all right, boy. Take it easy. My name's Markham. I've been hotel doctor here for eighteen years, but nothing of this sort has ever— Tell me," he broke off, "was there some rival suitor who might have—? It's the work of a deranged person, obviously. A—a sex maniac, with marked sadistic tendencies. I don't recommend," he added gently, "that your wife be moved for a few days. She's...she's been very badly mauled. No serious injury; mostly shock. But—is there anyone you'd like me to notify?"

"No! Yes! My uncle, Walter Ferris, curator of the state museum," Bob blurted out distractedly, running a hand through his hair. "Oh, why, why did I leave her, even for a few minutes?" he groaned. "She just seemed to want a minute alone, like most brides. And I—I—"

The doctor laid a hand on his shoulder. "Of course," he said kindly, but with a wary look in his eyes. "Now, my boy, tell me—do you ever suffer from—intense headaches? Er—loss of memory? Recurrent nightmares, in which you—?"

Bob Hanson jerked up his head, glaring at him.

"Good lord!" he gasped. "You think *I* did this to poor Celia? That I'm a—a mental case, and just don't remember having...?

But I do remember!" he insisted helplessly. "We talked about the view, and having our dinner sent up. Then I...I went down after a pack of cigarettes, because Celia wanted to undress—"

"Yes," Dr. Markham said quietly. "But—the desk clerk tells me you were up here with your young bride for almost an hour, before you came down to the lobby alone. Looking rather nervous, one of the porters said." He smiled. "Of course, that's natural for a groom. Still—" The smile faded.

Bob gaped at him, his straightforward blue eyes flinching before the older man's expression.

"But I—I couldn't have! How could I?" He strode over to the doctor, and seized his shoulders as though they were the only solid things in the hotel room. "Doctor! I...was thrown from a pony once, as a child. I struck my head. Could that have...?"

"It's possible," the physician nodded gently, then noted the raising agitation in the young man's face. "Now, now. We'll straighten this out later—you've had a terrible shock. Suppose you take the room next to mine for tonight, eh? In the morning we'll— Odd-looking ring you have there," he changed the subject smoothly in an effort to wipe some of the horror from the bridegroom's eyes. "Very ancient, isn't it? I collect ancient objects," he went on talking pleasantly. "Have a genuine scarab, from the tomb of Rameses. And a Mayan idol—hideous little thing. Mind if I look at that?"

Bob Hanson glanced down at his hand dully, which was still clutching the Babylonian ring his uncle had given his bride. The doctor took it from his nerveless grasp and turned it over and over, examining the tiny fragment of cloth-like stuff set in the secret compartment.

"By George!" he murmured. "Interesting! A hair ring! Early Babylonian, from the looks of that cuneiform inscription." He talked on in a low soothing tone, edging Bob Hanson from the room where his young bride lay, half-conscious and battered.

Skillfully he steered the stunned young man to a room opened by the porter. Bob sank down on the bed, gulping gratefully at the brandy flask that Markham held to his lips.

Then, once more, he buried his face in his hands.

"Celia!" he groaned. "Just a sweet innocent. Why, she's barely eighteen! I don't suppose she's even kissed more than a couple of boys in her life, at church picnics or the like! We grew up together. I—I wouldn't hurt her for anything in the world!"

THE doctor sighed. In contrast to the clean-cut young man on the bed, he looked tired and wrinkled, with sober dark eyes that had seen a great deal of human suffering. Also, he had seen a deal of criminal insanity, having been resident at a state asylum for several years. He eyed Bob warily, watching the way his fingers twisted together like writhing snakes.

"Don't worry," he soothed. "The house detective has been posted outside your wife's door. Nothing else can…harm her tonight. But I think it best that you sleep here, until some investigation of this…this business has been made. I'm sure," he added keenly, "that you would not want a recurrence, if it turns out that you are subject to attacks of schizophrenia. Split personality, you understand. A Dr. Jekyll and Mr. Hyde personality."

The young man groaned again, and shook his head violently. "But I'm *not!* I remember *everything!* Somebody must have forced entrance—"

"No. No, that's impossible, Mr. Hanson. I've already checked."

Bob looked up, startled by the cold gravity of the doctor's voice.

"No." The older man destroyed his last hope, as mercifully as he could. "A maid was mopping the hall outside your room, during the entire time you say you were in the lobby and your wife was alone. No one—*no intruder*—could have entered the room in your absence, without being seen by the maid. And it's obvious that no one could gain entrance by way of that balcony. It's a drop of fifty feet—to the treetops!"

As his quiet words sank in, Bob's eyes widened in shock and incredulity. His neatly brushed head moved weakly from side to side in denial. Then, at the doctor's heavy shrug, he threw himself face down on the bed, his broad shoulders wracked by silent sobs.

"All right," he said brokenly. "Notify my uncle, please. He'll…take whatever steps you think necessary. Have me—committed, and send somebody to come and take Celia home."

About midnight, after young Hanson had drifted into a troubled sleep induced by strong sedatives, the doctor tiptoed from his room, carrying with him the heavy ring Bob had slipped from his bride's bruised hand.

DR. MARKHAM shook his head. It was a strange case, and a tragic one for everyone concerned. Ironically, he read the romantic inscription on the bride's betrothal ring, picking out the queer wedged-shaped symbols in a heavy tome on his desk. *"Mine through eternity…"* The physician grunted. There seemed nothing he could do tomorrow except commit that nice young boy to a mental hospital, after first notifying their families of his brutal attack on his young bride.

Sighing, Markham sat down at his desk, idly examining the massive ring as he mulled over the problem. The metal was very dark, a weird *pulsing* black that seemed to expand and billow like smoke. Curiously he brushed a drop of acid across one of the six flat outer sides, and discovered it to contain some gold and iron, also another metal that defied his knowledge. Slipping open the secret compartment, the doctor stared for a moment at the tiny bit of fabric framed inside, with its fine silken woof and dark coarse warp.

On impulse, opening his penknife, he gouged out a strand of each, and placed them under his microscope. They were, as he suspected, hair—but a strange combination. The yellow silky strand was human hair, he found. But the dark coarse filament was that of some animal, perhaps a dog or an ape. Markham, who had expected the interwoven locks of some ancient lovers, was nonplussed at this discovery. He resolved to tell young Hanson about that in the morning—then reminded himself wryly that, in view of the events, that combination of human-and-beast hair in the betrothal ring was all too appropriate.

Then, abruptly, his eyes narrowed. A crazy idea had popped into his head, so fantastic that he dared not mention it to anyone.

Leaping up from his chair, the doctor mounted the stairs to the floor above and entered the room of the young bride, after nodding casually to the house detective who dozed outside the door, on guard. Markham sat down quietly by the bed, checking the girl's pulse and frowning over the bruises and welts on her neck and shoulders.

Then, carefully, he slipped the massive ring on her finger, and waited. He did not have to wait long.

Almost instantly, the girl's calm expression changed to one of feverish excitement, ecstasy mingled with fear, horror, and revulsion. She began to toss and mutter in her sleep, and Markham had to bend close to catch her words—an odd combination of English and what he recognized finally as Sumerian, the ancient language of Babylonia!

"Ai! Phogor!" the girl whimpered. "Come! *E-Im-Khur-sag*...the high places in the wind! The winding stair shall lift me up to...chammanim...*Ai! Bel-peor! Thy handmaiden...awaits thy...pleasure....!*"

Celia cried out suddenly—and before Markham's startled eyes, a great red welt began to rise up on the flesh of her slim neck. Another appeared on her bare shoulder as she whimpered and cried out once more.

The doctor mopped his forehead, on which cold sweat had broken out. Dimly, though the night outside was still and clear, he thought he heard a rushing sound, as of a strong wind blowing. Through and beneath it, also, he heard a deep guttural voice, with the suggestion of words—hideous, lecherous words that blasphemed the very air of the room. Markham gulped, and bending quickly, withdrew the ring from Celia's finger—the ring which already had contracted and made a deep imprint on her flesh.

"Good God!" the doctor breathed shakily. "I...I never thought I'd have the privilege of seeing a genuine case. Stigmata! Hysterical stigmata! No question of it... But what brought it on?"

HE RAN his fingers over the welts and bruises on Celia's body, and pursed his lips in a soundless whistle of amazement. Some of the wounds were actually bleeding! And her fingernails, which had a moment before clawed frantically at the open air above her, were broken as though in struggle against some solid object. Looking closer at them, Markham opened his penknife and pried something out from beneath one nail. A hair! A dark coarse hair, exactly like that he had found in the ring. But perhaps Celia Hanson, too, had examined that secret compartment before her strange attack occurred.

Returning to his quarters, Dr. Markham sat for some time, poring over the big tomes in his library; reference works that pertained to his hobby of collecting ancient relics. Toward dawn he dozed off, his mind awhirl with strange conjectures— only to waken sharply with the feeling that someone was in his room.

Markham turned his head slightly where it rested on his desk. A hand was groping stealthily in the drawer near him, rummaging among his medicines. It selected a vial on the label of which a grinning skull warned of the dangerous contents.

The doctor leaped up, seizing the hand and knocking the bottle to the floor. With an expert twist, he forced young Bob Hanson into a chair and kicked the vial of poison out of reach under his bed. The boy glared at him hopelessly, slumped in his chair.

"Why did you stop me," he muttered, "after what I did? And it must have been I, if nobody else could get in that room.

Oh, don't you see? I've got to release Celia. She'd wait for me. She'd try to forgive me, to understand. Don't you see it's the only way for us now?"

"Except," Markham interrupted crisply, "to look at the facts, and use a little common sense and imagination. Relax, boy," he said softly. "It wasn't you. I didn't see how it could be—you've no symptoms of mental disorder. But—"

Bob's eyes widened. He jumped up from his chair. "They've caught him? The—the man who—?"

"There was no man," Markham said, patting his shoulder. "My young friend, I have every reason to believe that your bride's wounds and bruises are—stigmatic. That is, induced by hysteria and self-hypnosis. It's a medical phenomenon you don't see once in a lifetime. Though there was a case in the papers recently, a Theresa Neumann, who repeats the wounds of Christ on the cross every Good Friday. There was another case in the village of Vilar Chao, Portugal, a girl named Amelia. A cross appeared on her forehead in a great red welt when she said her Rosary.

"There are other kinds of stigmata, though, besides those caused by religious fervor. There was a Polish girl, Eleanor Zugun, who would break out in welts and scratches when she believed a spirit-creature, a poltergeist, was attacking her. Her hands were tied and she was watched by a group of physicians, but the welts would appear just the same—dreadful raw, red wounds on her cheek or neck."

Young Hanson blinked at him, utterly bewildered. "But," he blurted, "you don't mean that Celia—? Why, she's not the hysterical type. Are you saying now that she, not I, is the mental case?"

The gray-haired physician stared back at him, his own eyes dark with bewilderment.

"Perhaps," he said quietly, "my medical report will say that your young bride subconsciously feared marriage, though consciously she trusted and loved her new husband. Psychiatry. We scientists," he smiled wryly, "are willing to accept its strange ins and outs as medical fact. But— I personally believe," he added slowly, "that this is a *psychical* phenomenon. Mr. Hanson, I believe that, for the short period you left your wife alone in that room in her highly emotional state, she became hypersensitive to…what the American Society for Psychic Research calls *psychometry.*"

"Psychomety?" Bob Hanson repeated, amazed. "Say, I've heard of that. There were some recent tests made at Harvard in extra-sensory perception. It's the opposite of clairvoyance, isn't it? A psychometry medium can take some object in his hand and sense its past—or events that happened closely connected with the object?"

Markham nodded. "Precisely. I've observed one such medium in her—call it 'trance', if you like. A lady, a chubby palmist who plied her trade in a tent outside Miami. She was actually able to take a piece of ordinary brickbat in her hand and describe the details of a murder committed with it. She even drew a clear picture of the murderer. He was later convicted of the crime—though not on such flimsy legal evidence as a psychometric reading. Our authorities are not inclined to credit these matters. But 'thoughts are things', as the saying goes. They impregnate metal and wood and stone, much as radioactive heat does in a certain area. Everyone can sense such waves at times, especially in moments of intense emotion. But some of us are more receptive than others, more intense.

"Mr. Hanson," the doctor finished flatly, "I believe your wife is such a person and that she relived an experience strongly attached to this ancient Babylonian ring you gave her. You call it a betrothal ring, and it is just that—but in a rather ghastly way."

The doctor shuddered visibly, then went on:

"I examined the cuneiform inscription very carefully. A sinister one, rather than romantic. Coupled with what your wife muttered in her sleep when I slipped the ring on her finger, I believe the thing to be the betrothal ring of a young bride of ancient Babylonia. A virgin bride of the city of Peor, on the Tigris.

"There was, as you may know, a religious custom among those who worshipped the god Baal—or Bel is the Babylonian word, meaning *lord* or *possessor*. An evil, vicious custom. Directly after a wedding the young bride was required to sit in the temple and give herself to the first stranger who tossed a handful of silver into her lap. She could not refuse to submit herself to the first comer—even if he happened to be a leprous beggar. Then, and only then, could the bride go to her lawful husband. A practice so unthinkable that the Canaanites came to speak of the god as 'shame-lord' or *'Baal-ze-bub'*, the 'god of flies'.

"The stranger, of course, represented Bel. A shaggy filthy monster with a beast's body and the old lewd face of a man. But sometimes, if the young bride was very fair and innocent, the god himself came to claim first fruits, as the practice was called."

Bob Hanson, listening intently, tugged at his collar as the import of Markham's words reached him all at once.

"And—Celia?" he forced out the name. "She—she—?"

"...relived the experience of that young bride of Peor," the doctor nodded grimly. "By the medium of psychometry. A truly horrible experience. No wonder her physical body was affected to the extent of stigmatic wounds. Of all the impious deities of antiquity, Bel, or Baal, was known and despised for his obscene brutality. Most of our Christian prophets preached against him, and burned down his temples—Daniel, Isaiah, Jeremiah. They weren't exaggerating when they called the rites of Bel an 'abomination!'"

Young Hanson shivered uncontrollably. "Oh, my poor Celia," he moaned. "Of course, she'll have to be hospitalized. But I'll wait for her. I'll—I'll help her forget this terrible experience if it takes the rest of my life."

Dr. Markham smiled, slapping him on the back gently.

"But it won't take that long," he said cheerfully. "Unless I'm much mistaken—" He glanced out the window to where the sun was rising, clear and warm, over the mountain ridge. "In fact, I rather think your pretty bride is waking up right now, hungry for breakfast—and worried about where you are. Shall we go up to see her?"

The young man nodded eagerly, and in a moment the two men were standing beside Celia's bed. She stared at Markham, pulling up the covers modestly over the torn negligee. Then, as he took her wrist with a faint smile, she relaxed; making a little face at Bob.

"Oh—you're a doctor? Good heavens! Did I faint or something last night? Poor Bob! He must have been frantic, to call in a..." She moaned faintly, sinking back on her pillow. "But I do feel awful! And those horrible nightmares—!" The bride's face convulsed with horror, then flushed to the roots of her hair. "It—it was that dog-thing I thought I saw at the wedding! Ugh! It came to me, and—I was terrified, and yet—" She rolled her head from side to side as though in an effort to dispel the confused memory. "Oh, it's all mixed up!"

Bob moved quickly to the bedside, and she took his hand in both of hers, smiling shakily.

"Oh, darling," Celia apologized, "I didn't mean to frighten you. But I...I felt as though I'd been drugged. I couldn't wake up. Just kept on and on dreaming about this...this strange ancient-looking city. There was a crowd in the streets, around a great tall building. Some robed men were dancing in a sort of queer *limp*. Then..." She shuddered. "Then one of them snatched a poor little baby from its mother and...and dashed its brains out on a big six-sided stone! Oh, it was horrible! But I couldn't wake up...

"Then a...a young girl, with a wreath of flowers on her head. I... It seemed to be *me!* There was a long flight of stone steps winding around the outside of that tall tower. I climbed and climbed, with those people howling below me. Then there was a door opening. And a big room, lighted with a weird green glow; a room with simply dreadful pictures on the tiled walls. They...they made me blush. Then there was a huge couch, all gold and blue jewels, piled high with pillows. And the wind—it blew and howled all the time. Then...I...I..."

Celia stopped, then plunged on, her breath coming in short gasps of horror.

"I...looked up, and that *Thing* was coming toward me, talking in a horrible guttural voice and...*and reaching for me!"*

SHE gave a little moan and buried her face in the pillow. Over her head Bob Hanson looked despairingly at Dr. Markham. But the doctor shook his head. Lightly, he flipped back the cover to reveal the girl's bare shoulders and neck, which had been covered with such dreadful bruises.

Young Hanson stared, unbelieving. The wounds had disappeared! He raised his eyes once more to Markham's, lips parted. But again the wise old physician shook his head, moving unostentatiously toward the door.

"We are all troubled by nightmares and nervousness," he said soothingly. "I wouldn't be too upset by it, young lady. Just take it easy for the next few days—and enjoy your honeymoon! You'll be fine as soon as you and this anxious young man of yours have had breakfast together. I'll drop in later. Much later!"

He closed the door after him, smiling, and strode down the hall to return to his own quarters. The ring, the evil ring of Belpeor, was still in his pocket—to be mailed back to Walter Ferris with the full story, at young Hanson's request. Bob could pretend to have lost it. Anything, so that it would never again close, vise-like, about his bride's slim finger—as it had closed about the finger of that other young bride of Peor, many centuries before Christ.

Markham frowned. There was much about this case that he simply did not understand—and much that he did not care to understand. That dark coarse hair in the secret compartment of the ring, for instance—with its counterpart under Celia's fingernail. That could be explained, perhaps, in a natural way—

But he could not explain the fact that the silky blond strands interwoven with it were, under his microscope, identical to the hair on Celia Hanson's head—though it had been set into that ancient Babylonian ring over three thousand years ago!

THE END

ROOM WITH A VIEW

By Esther Carlson

*You find them in New York, mostly in the rabbit warrens below
Fourteenth Street. Youngsters who dream of writing the Great
American Novel, of singing the title role in Rigoletto, or of out-smearing
Picasso. They dine at Nedicks, browse in dusty shops, and their only
real talent is the ability to dream.
Some of them, like the hero of Esther Carlson's astringent little story,
find only one remedy for their frustrations—one more dramatic than their
dreams...*

THERE once was a poor young artist named Bosco
Blossom who lived sixth floor rear of a dreadful rooming house
on West Seventeenth.

Bosco had a Renoir soul but the convictions of a cubist and
his paintings showed a kind of square romanticism that was not
in demand. This strange schizophrenia also had an effect on his
social life; those whom he could love he could not agree with,
and those with whom he could agree gave him the shudders.
Consequently Bosco was not only poor, he was lonely.

One fine spring day, however, Bosco worked two miracles;
he created a masterpiece, and he filled his life with joy.

Bosco was pacing up and down his room, brush in hand,
blank canvas all around him, seething with youth and spring and
unable to do anything about it, like a bird with a band on its
beak.

Finally he cast himself upon the cot and moaned: "A scrap
of blue! A fragment of cloud... That's all I ask. Is it too
much?"

The object of Bosco's dismay was his window, and a fitting
object it was indeed. It was the only window in the narrow
room and it opened to a vast expanse of ugly brick, the blind

slab side of the neighboring warehouse. Below six stories was a filthy court.

"How *can* I be inspired?" Bosco cried out to his fates bitterly. "Give me a room with a view!"

He hung his head over the side of the bed and stared down at his splotched and dried-up palette.

"And you," he said crazily. *"You* would look like a damned Venetian sunset!"

It was only a figure of speech, but it contained an idea. "A Venetian sunset," Bosco repeated thoughtfully. "And what if I had splashed these colors on that vile brick wall... What if..."

Bosco ran down his six flights to the street, sprinted into the hardware store, bought a bamboo pole, ran up again, sat on his cot, and began to think.

He discarded Rio; he considered the Rockettes' dressing room; he gave much thought to the Alps by moonlight. Intellectually he scorned a pleasant daisied meadow; emotionally he could not stand the three-dimensioned, perfect pyramids. Then he examined his painting materials and found nothing but tubes of blue and green and white.

"That settles it," Bosco said. "I'll do a blue nude on a green pony. Anything's better than brick."

With that he tied the brush on the end of his bamboo pole and painted his picture on the part of the warehouse just across from his window.

When his colors ran out, he clambered in off the ledge and stood back for the effect. It was overwhelming.

For what Bosco had painted was the sea-green sea, lit by a bright day, moved by a brisk wind. Delicate white caps broke into chartreuse foam; aquamarine became limpid azure, the horizon shimmered afar off in a filmy mist. The unevenness of the worn bricks lent undulation to the water, gave it sweep to Spain.

"My God," breathed Bosco. "Sheer genius!"

He was unable to do anything the whole day but stare out his window at the vista. Though he had promised himself a walk in the Square, he could not leave his view. The dancing waves lapped against his windowsill and the movements of the city boomed in like distant surf.

Toward evening his landlady came up the stairs to the sixth floor room, panting the while like a freight engine on a steep grade.

"Blossom," she snorted outside the door. "Rent due."

Bosco returned to reality long enough to shove six worn-out dollar bills under the door.

"Whatcha got in there?" she said. "A girl?"

"No, ma'am," said Bosco.

"Huh," she said, and departed.

Bosco felt a little sick but he consoled himself, for now that he had his view his brush would stroke out pictures of divine reason and beauty and pretty girls and fine fellows would say to him:

"Come, Bosco, we are having a party tonight. We all want you to come." Of course!

He dreamed, and for weeks he scarcely took his eyes off the window except to go down the hall, as one must do in rooming houses, or to rush to Nedick's for a quick cheese sandwich. In the early morning the aspect of the sea was fresh and new; by noon the swells grew rounder, heavier. Dusk gave the water a leaden, ominous, exciting power, but night found it sheathed in sheer loveliness. The glare of the city's lights could not touch Bosco's view; instead, a glow from above seemed to diffuse over it, tingeing the crests with cool silver. He was content. His was the ever-changing, never-changing sea.

That is, he was content for a while. One morning in early summer he began to pace the floor.

"Look at this hideous, mouse-gnawed hole!" he cried. "How unbecoming. How unseemly. Though my view inspires me to the greatest degree, the moment I take my eyes away from it and pick up my brush, alas, I am surrounded by scabby brown walls, a tipsy couch, a pot-bellied dresser! How can I release my Art in such an interior?" And life was ruined until he received his second great idea.

He painted his room.

He painted his room white. Not for nothing had Bosco once seen the saloon of a yacht. Very lifelike on the walls he drew lifesavers; he strung ropes around with his brush and, with an orange crate and a bit of judicious hammering so as not to arouse his landlady, he turned his cot into a bunk. He did not fashion portholes. There was only one porthole, and it had the view.

So exquisite was his workmanship, so life-like in every detail that his easel with its empty canvas seemed a jarring note and he tucked them under the bunk and stowed his art materials aft. That night as he lay in his cabin listening to the crashing breakers of the city-sea, the mewing cries of the taxi-gulls, he felt the gentle sway of the boat under his frail body. The lash of the rain woke him in the morning and through it dimly he saw his oily sea swelling, rolling, and when the Queen Mary boomed in the harbor it seemed only natural for Bosco to reach up, pull an imaginary cord and give her an answering call.

During the midsummer storms Bosco acquired sea legs and not even the lurching of his vessel in the heaving waters threw him to the deck. Then there were the calm days and nights when the boat steered effortlessly on her course and he needed to do nothing but lie on his bunk and dream. It was great fun, and one day he went ashore and with his last three dollar bills purchased a yachting cap.

The transition from his cabin to the hallway and the ordinary sounds, sights and odors of life in a rooming house became almost more than Bosco could bear. In his boat he could sniff the fresh salt air; in the hall it was cabbage. The thought of his landlady caused him to shiver, she who lurked in the slimy depths like a sea monster waiting to devour him and his flimsy craft.

"To hell with this," Bosco told himself. "I'll take my yacht to the South Seas. Anchors aweigh!" And he locked himself in his cabin, cast off and took her out.

Once when he was hungry he let a line out of his porthole. Some joker downstairs put a sardine on it and Bosco hauled it up and ate it for supper. And all the time it got warmer and warmer, for August was upon the city, and the sea.

Bosco felt the tropical breeze on his cheek. "I should be sighting land soon," he mused. To make certain of it he found his bamboo pole, resurrected his paint brush and green paint and put, on his horizon, a palm-fringed island.

But though the days and nights stretched on and there was not a breath of air, the island drew no closer. Bosco really didn't expect it to; he was not utterly mad.

"Becalmed," he repeated over and over, shaking his head, conscious that his position was dangerous. The monster would crawl up from her lair at any moment to overwhelm himself and his helpless craft.

There came a still, moon-lit August evening when the sea was calm and awash with silver. In the quiet Bosco heard her coming up—up—up till she was pounding at his door.

"Blossom! Blossom!"

He did not answer.

"I know you're there, Blossom. Three weeks rent you're owing."

Bosco lay stiff with loathing; the cabin reeked of her foul cabbage breath and he could feel her sneering eye stripping his dream of the magic paint, so that the view became once again but ugly brick and the scab brown walls of his former room.

"I'm coming back in an hour," she hissed. "I'll get this door open. I know your kind…"

Coming back! Bosco cringed. "Anyway," he said aloud. "Anyway, by God, I'll have a revel my last night on board."

From under his bunk he pulled his emergency stores: a bottle of grog, stowed for many a week and unnecessary, for the young sailor had been drunk of the sea air and imagination. He watched his waving palm trees in the distance and moodily swigged from the bottle.

"Room with a view," he said. "Farewell. Good-bye."

Suddenly the floor tipped, the craft surged forward, the bunk swayed under him. Bosco sat up, staring at his view. He was drawing closer to the island! He *was!* The trees *were* closer, more distinct. Yes, he could almost distinguish a sandy beach out there in the moonlight and closer...closer. He peered, squinting his eyes. On the beach were people, girls running about, playing. He could almost hear the laughter. He yearned for them and for the soft sand beneath his toes.

"Hurry!" he cried, tossing down the grog. "Hurry and we'll make her. Faster. Faster."

Beautiful girls, long dark hair, dancing on the beach. Clumping outside, cabbage smells, drawing near, crawling toward him...

"Give her all she's got, Mr. Engineer," he hollered down the bottle neck. "Full speed ahead!"

Louder came the clumping, mutterings outside his cabin door. Bosco downed the last of the liquid and took off his clothes.

A pounding began on the door. "Blossom. I'm coming in!"

"What do I care?" Bosco shouted. "I can make it now!"

And as she battered down his cabin door, Bosco dove from the porthole into the deep dark sea.

THE END

I'M LOOKING FOR JEFF

By Fritz Leiber

*Years ago, murder in fiction was done by gentle people and was solved when
the Inspector learned that Aunt Fanny's lorgnette lay twelve degrees east of
the old sundial. Then one day an author came along and took murder out
of the rose garden—and the detective story was popular again.
The same goes for horror tales. Where once ghosts haunted baronial halls
and got all tangled up in the cobwebs on Lord Poopdeck's armor, they now
hang around the neighborhood candy store and the corner saloon. Horror in
familiar surroundings in far more effective, we think; for nothing could be
quite so blood curdling as a familiar familiar!*

AT Six-thirty that afternoon, Martin Bellows was sitting at
the bar of the Tomtoms. In front of him was a tall glass of beer
and behind the bar were two men in white aprons. The two
men, one of them so old he was past caring about it, were
discussing a matter—and while Martin wasn't really listening,
much of the discussion seemed to be for his entertainment.

"If that girl comes in again I won't serve her. And if she
starts to get funny I'll give her some real eye-shadow!"

"Regular fire eater, aren't you, Pops?"

"All this week, ever since she started to come in here, there's
been trouble."

"Listen to him, will you? Aw, Pops, there's always trouble at
a bar. Either somebody makes a play for somebody's girl, or
else it's two life-long buddies—"

"I mean nasty trouble. What about those two girls Monday
night? What about what the big guy did to Jack? What about
Jake and Janice picking the Tomtoms to break up, and the way
they did it? *She* was behind it every time. What about the
broken glass in the cracked ice?"

"Shut up! Pops is nuts, friend. He gets wild ideas."

Martin Bellows looked up from his beer at Sol, the young

115

working owner of the Tomtoms, and at the other man behind the bar. Then he glanced down the empty stretch of polished mahogany and over his shoulder at the dim, silent stretches of the booths, where the lights from behind the bar hardly picked up the silver and gilt. He grimaced faintly.

"Anything for a little life."

"Life!" Pops snorted. "That isn't what she'd give you, Mister."

There's no lonelier place in the world than a nightspot in the early hours of evening. It makes one think of all the guys who are alone—without a girl or a friend—restlessly searching. Its noiseless gloom is a sounding board for the faintest fears and aches of the heart. Its atmosphere, used to being pushed around by the loud mouths of happy drunks, is stagnant. The dark corners that should be filled with laughter and desire are ghostly. The bandstand, with the empty chairs sitting around in lifelike positions.

Martin felt it and hitched his stool an inch closer to the old man and the anxious, sharp-eyed Sol.

"Tell me about her, Pops," he said to the old man. "No, let him, Sol."

"All right, but I'm warning you it's a pipe dream."

Pops ignored his boss's remark. He spun the glass he was polishing in a slower rhythm. His face puffed by beer and thumbed into odd hills and gullies by a lifetime of evanescent but illuminating experiences, grew thoughtful. Outside traffic moaned and a distant train hooted. Pops pressed his lips together, bringing out a new set of hummocks in his cheeks.

"Name's Bobby," he began abruptly. "Blonde. About twenty. Always orders brandies. Smooth kid face, except for the faintest scar that goes all the way across it. Black dress that splits down to her belly-button."

A car slammed to a stop outside. The three men looked up. But after a moment they heard the car go on.

"Never set eyes on her till last Sunday night," Pops

continued. "Says she's from Michigan City. Always asking for a guy named Jeff. Always waiting to start her particular kind of hell."

"Who's this Jeff?" Martin asked.

Pops shrugged.

"And what's her particular kind of hell?"

Pops shrugged again, this time in Sol's direction. "He don't believe in her," he said gruffly.

"I'd like to meet her, Pops," Martin said smilingly. "Like some excitement. Beginning to feel a big evening coming on. And Bobby sounds like my kind of girl."

"I wouldn't introduce her to my last year's best friend!"

Sol laughed lightly but conclusively. He leaned across the bar, confidentially, glancing back at the older man with secretive humor. He touched Martin's sleeve. "You've heard Pops' big story. Now get this: I've never been able to notice this girl, and I'm always here until I close. So far as I know, nobody's ever been able to notice her except Pops. I think she's just one of his pipe dreams. You know, the guy's a little weak in the head." He leaned a bit closer and spoke in a loud and mocking stage whisper, "*Used weed when he was a boy.*"

Pops' face grew a bit red, and the new set of hummocks stood out more sharply. "All right, Mr. Wise," he said. "I got something for you."

He put the glass down in the shining ranks, hung up the towel, fished a cigar box from under the bar.

"Last night she forgot her lighter," he explained. "It's covered with a dull, shiny black stuff, same as her dress... Look!"

The other two men leaned forward, but when Pops flipped up the cover there was nothing inside but the white paper lining.

Sol looked around at Martin with a slow grin. "You see?"

Pops swore and ripped out the lining. "One of the band must have swiped it!"

Sol laid his hand gently on the older man's arm. "Our musicians are nice, honest boys, Pops."

"But I tell you I put it there last thing last night."

"No, Pops, you just thought you did." He turned to Martin. "Not that strange things don't sometimes happen in bars. Why, just these last few days—"

A door slammed. The three men looked around. But it must have been a car outside, for nothing came in.

"Just these last few days," Sol repeated, "I've been noticing the damndest thing."

"What?" Martin asked.

Sol shot another of his secretively humorous glances toward Pops. "I'd like to tell you," he explained to Martin, "but I can't in front of Pops. He gets ideas."

Martin got off his stool, grinning. "I got to go anyhow. I'll see you later."

Not five minutes later, Pops smelled the perfume. A rotten, sickly smell. And his ears caught the mouse-faint creaking of the midmost barstool, and the tiny, ghostly sigh. And the awful feel of it went deep down inside him and grated on his bones like chalk. He began to tremble.

Then the creaking and the sigh came again through the gloom of the Tomtoms, a little impatiently, and he had to turn, although it was the last thing he wanted to do, and he had to look at the emptiness of the bar. And there, at the midmost stool, he saw it.

It was terribly indistinct, just a shadowy image superimposed on the silvers and gilts and midnight blues of the far wall, but he knew every part of it. The gleaming blackness of the dress, like the sheerest black silk stocking held up in near darkness. The pale gold of the hair, like motes in the beam of an amber spotlight. The paleness of face and hands, like puffs of powder floating up from a spilled compact. The eyes, like two tiny dark moths, hovering.

"What's the matter, Pops?" Sol asked sharply.

He didn't hear the question. Although he'd have given anything not to have to do it, he was edging shakily down the bar, hand grasping the inner margin for support, until he stood before the midmost stool.

Then he heard it, the faint clear voice that seemed to ride a mosquito's whine, as they say the human voice rides a radio wave. The voice that knifed deep, deep into his head.

"Been talking about me, Pops?"

He just trembled.

"Seen Jeff tonight, Pops?"

He shook his head.

"What's the matter, Pops? What if I'm dead and rotting? Don't shake so, Pops, you've got the wrong build for a shimmy dancer. You should be complimented I show myself to you. You know, Pops, at heart every woman's a stripper. But most of them just show themselves to the guy they like, or need. I'm that way. I don't show myself to the bums. And now give me a drink."

His trembling only increased.

The twin moths veered toward him. "Got polio, Pops?"

In a spasm of haste he jerked around, stooping. By blind fumbling he found the brandy bottle under the ranked glasses, poured a shaky shot, set it down on the bar and stepped back.

"What the hell are you up to?"

He didn't even hear the angry question, or realize that Sol was moving toward him. Instead, he stood pressed back as far as he could, and watched the powder cloud fingers wind around the shot glass like tendrils of smoke, and heard the bat-shrill voice laugh ruefully and say, "Can't manage it that way, haven't got strength enough yet," and watched the twin moths, and something red and white-edged just below them, dip toward the brandy.

Then for a moment a feeling reached out and touched Sol, for though no hand was on the bar, the shot glass shook, and a little rill of brandy snaked down its side and pooled on the mahogany.

"What the…" Sol began and then finished, "Those damn trucks, they shake the whole neighborhood."

And all the while Pops was listening to the bat-shrill voice: "That helped, Pops," and then with a wheedling restlessness, "What's on tonight, Pops? Where can a girl get herself some fun? Who was the tall, dark and handsome that left a while ago? You called him Martin?"

Sol, finally fed up, came striding toward Pops. "And now you'll please explain just what the—"

"Wait!" Pops hand snapped out and clamped on Sol's arm so that the younger man winced. "She's getting up," he gasped. "She's going after him. We got to warn him."

Sol's sharp gaze quickly flashed where Pops was looking. Then, with a little snarl, he shook off Pops' hand and gripped him in turn. "Look here, Pops, are you really smoking weed?"

The older man struggled to free himself. "We got to warn him. I tell you, before she drinks herself strong enough to make him notice her, and starts putting her broken-bottle ideas into his head."

"Pops!" The shout in the ear stiffened the older man, so that he stood there quietly, though rigid, while Sol said, "They probably have some nut bars out on West Madison Street they don't mind having nuts behind. Probably. I don't know. But you're going to have to start looking for one of them if you pull any more of these goofy acts, or start talking about any Bobby and broken glass." His fingers kneaded the old man's biceps. "Get it?"

Pops' eyes were still wild. But he nodded twice, stiffly.

The evening started out feeling heavy and indigestible for Martin Bellows, but after a while it began to float like the diamond-dusted clouds of light around the street lamps. The session with Pops and Sol had given him a funny sort of edge, but he rode out the mood, drifting from tavern to tavern, occasionally treating a decent-looking guy to a drink and letting himself be treated in turn, sharing that courtesy silently, not talking very much, kidding a bit with the girls behind the bars while he covertly eyed the ones in front. After about five taverns and eight drinks he found he'd picked up one of them.

She was a small willowy girl with hair like a winter sunrise and a sleekly-fitting black dress, high-necked but occasionally revealing a narrow ribbon of sweet flesh. Her eyes were dark and friendly, and not exactly law-abiding, and her face had the smooth, matte quality of pale doeskin. He was aware of a faint gardenia perfume. He put his arm around her and kissed her lightly, under the street lamp, not closing his eyes, and as he did so he noticed that her face had a blemish. The tiniest line of paler flesh, like a single strand of spider web, began at her left temple and went straight across the lids of her left eye and the bridge of her nose and back across the right cheek. It enhanced her beauty, he thought.

"Where'll we go?" he asked.

"How about the Tomtoms?"

"A little too early." Then, "Say! Your name is Bobby. That's the name Pops...I'll bet you're..."

She shrugged. "Pops likes to talk."

"Sure you are! Pops was spieling about you at a great rate." He smiled at her fondly. "Claims you're an evil influence."

"Yes?"

"But don't worry about that. Pops is stark, raving nuts. Why, only this evening—"

"Well, let's go some place else," she interrupted. "I need a drink, lover."

And they were off, Martin with his heart singing, because what you always look for and never find had actually happened to him: he had found a girl that set his imagination and his thirst aflame. Every minute made him more desirous and prouder of her. Bobby was the perfect girl, he decided. She didn't get loud, or quarrelsome, or complaining, or soul-baring, or full of supposedly cute, deliberately exasperating whims. Instead, she was gay and smooth and beautiful, fitting his mood like a glove, yet with that hint of danger and savagery that can never be divorced from the dizzy fumes of alcohol and the dark streets of cities. He found himself growing very foolish about her. He even came to dote on her spider-like scar, as if it were an expert repair job done on an expensive French doll.

They went to three or four delightful taverns, one where a gray-haired woman sang meltingly, one that showed silent comedies on a small screen instead of television, one full of framed pencil portraits of unknown, unimportant people. Martin got through all the early stages of intoxication—the eager, the uneasy, the dreamily blissful—and emerged safely into that crystal world where time almost stands still, where nothing is surer than your movements and nothing realer than your feelings, where the tight shell of personality is shattered and even dark walls and smoky sky and gray cement underfoot are sentient parts of you.

But after a while he kissed Bobby again, in the street, holding her longer and closer this time, plunging his lips to her neck, drowning in the autumn-garden sweetness of gardenia perfume, murmuring unsteadily, "You've got a place around here?"

"Yes."

"Well..."

"Not now, lover," she breathed. "First let's go to the Tomtoms."

He nodded and drew a bit back from her, not angrily.

"Who's Jeff?" he asked.

She looked up at him. "Do you want to know?"

"Yes."

"Look, lover," she said softly, "I don't think you'll ever meet Jeff. But if you do, I want you to promise me one thing—I won't ever ask for anything else." She paused, and all the latent savagery glowed in the pale mask of her features. "I want you to promise me that you'll break the bottom off a beer bottle and jam it into his fat face."

"What'd he do to you?"

The pale mask was enigmatic. "Something much worse than you're thinking," she told him.

Looking down at Bobby's still, expectant face, Martin felt a thrill of murderous excitement go through him.

"Promise?" she asked.

"Promise," he said huskily.

Sol was content only during the busy hours when life ran high in the Tomtoms. Lovers for an evening or forever, touching knees under the tables, meant money in the register.

Sol and Pops had had a busy two hours, but now there was a lull between jazz sessions and Sol had time to chew the rag a bit with a burly and interesting looking stranger.

"Talk about funny things, friend, here's one for you," he said, leaning across the bar with a confidential smile. "See that stool second on your left? Every night this week, after one a.m., nobody sits on it."

"It's empty now," the burly man told him.

"Sure, and the one next you. But I'm talking about after one a.m.—that's a couple of minutes yet—when our business hits its peak. No matter how big the crowd is— they could be standing two deep other places—nobody ever occupies that one stool. Why? I don't know. Maybe it's just chance. Maybe there's something funny I haven't figured out yet makes them sheer off from it."

"Just chance," the burly man opined stolidly. He had a fighter's jaw and a hooded gaze.

Sol smiled. Across the room the musicians were climbing back onto the bandstand, leisurely settling themselves. "Maybe, friend. But I got a feeling it's something else. Maybe something very obvious, like that it's got a leg that's a teensy bit loose. But I'm willing to bet it'll stay empty tonight. You watch. Six nights in a row is too good for just chance. And I'd swear on a stack of Bibles it's been empty six nights straight."

"That just ain't so, Sol."

Sol turned. Pops was standing behind him, eyes scared and angry like they'd been earlier, lips working a little.

"What do you mean, Pops?" Sol asked him, trying not to

123

show irritation in front of his new customer.

Pops walked off muttering.

"Got to see that the girls are taking care of the tables," Sol excused himself to the burly man and went after Pops. When he caught up with him he said in an undertone, not looking at him, "Damn it, Pops, are you just trying to make yourself unpleasant?" Across the room the bandleader stood up and smiled around at his boys. "If you think I'm going to take that kind of stuff from you, you're crazy."

"But, Sol," Pops' voice was quavery now, almost as if he were looking for protection, "there ain't ever been an empty place at the bar after one a.m. this week. And as for that particular stool—"

The humorous trumpet-bray opening the first number, spraying a ridicule of all pomp and circumstance across every square inch of the Tomtoms, cut him short.

"Yes?" Sol prompted.

But now Pops was no longer aware of him. It was one a.m. and across the smoky distance of the Tomtoms he was watching her come, materializing from the gloom of the entry, no longer a thing of smoke but strong with the night and the night's secret powers, solidly blocking off the first booths and the green of the dice-table as she passed them.

He noted without surprise or regret that she'd caught the nice boy she'd gone after, as she caught everything she went after. And now nearer and nearer—the towel dropped from Pops' fingers—past the bandstand, past the short, chromium-fenced stretch of bar where the girls got the drinks for the tables, until she spun herself up onto the midmost barstool and smiled cruelly at him. "'Lo, Pops."

The nice boy sat down next to her and said, "Two brandies, Pops. Soda chasers." Then he took out a pack of cigarettes, began to battle through his pockets for matches.

She touched his arm. "Get me my lighter, Pops," she said.

Pops shook.

She leaned forward a little. The smile left her face. "I said get me my lighter, Pops."

He ducked like a man being shot at. His numb hands found the cigar box under the bar. There was something small and black inside. He grabbed it up as if it were a spider and thrust it down blindly on the bar, jerked back his hand. Bobby picked it up and flicked her thumb and lifted a small yellow flame to the nice boy's cigarette. The nice boy smiled at her lovingly and then asked, "Hey, Pops, what about our drinks?"

For Martin, the crystal world was getting to be something of a china shop. Stronger and stronger, slowly and pleasurably working toward a climax like the jazz, he could feel the urge toward wild and happy action. Masculine action, straight-armed, knife-edged, dramatic, destroying or loving half to death everything around him. Waiting for the inevitable—whatever it was would be—he almost gloated.

The old man half spilled their drinks, he was in such a hurry setting them down. Pops really did seem a bit nuts, just like Sol had said, and Martin stopped the remark he'd half intended to make about finding Pops' girl. Instead, he looked at Bobby.

"You drink mine, lover," she said, leaning close to be heard over the loud music, and again he saw the scar. "I've had enough."

Martin didn't mind. The double brandy burned icily along his nerves, building higher the cool flame of savagery that was fanned by the band blaring derision at the haughty heads and high towers of civilization.

A burly man, who was taking up a little too much room beside Martin, caught Sol's attention as the latter passed inside the bar, and said, "So far you're winning. It's still empty." Sol nodded, smiled, and whispered some witticism. The burly man laughed, and in appreciation said a dirty word.

Martin tapped his shoulder. "I'll trouble you not to use that sort of language in front of my girl."

The burly man looked at him and beyond him, said, "You're drunk, Joe," and turned away.

Martin tapped his shoulder again. "I said I'd trouble you—"

"You will, Joe, if you keep it up," the burly man told him, keeping a poker face. "Where is this girl you're talking about? In the washroom? I tell you, Joe, you're drunk."

"She's sitting right beside me," Martin said, enunciating each word with care and staring grimly into the eyes of the poker face.

The burly man smiled. He seemed suddenly amused. "Okay, Joe," he said, "let's investigate this girl of yours. What's she like? Describe her to me."

"Why, you—" Martin began, drawing back his arm.

Bobby caught hold of it. "No, lover," she said in a curiously intent voice. "Do as he says."

"Why the devil—"

"Please, lover," she told him. She was smiling tightly. Her eyes were gleaming. "Do just as he says."

Martin shrugged. His own smile was tight as he turned back to the burly man. "She's about twenty. She's got hair like pale gold. She looks a bit like Veronica Lake. She's dressed in black and she's got a black cigarette lighter."

Martin paused. Something in the poker face had changed. Perhaps it was a shade less ruddy. Bobby was tugging at his arm.

"You haven't told him about the scar," she said excitedly.

He looked at her, frowning.

"Tell him about the scar too."

"Oh, yes," he said, "and she's got the faintest scar running down from her left temple over her left eyelid and the bridge of her nose, and across her right cheek to the lobe of her—"

He stopped abruptly. The poker face was ashen, its lips were working. Then a red tide started to flood up into it, the eyes began to look murder.

Martin could feel Bobby's warm breath in his ear, the flick of her wet tongue. "Now, lover. Get him now. That's Jeff."

Swiftly, yet very deliberately, Martin shattered the rim of his chaser glass against the shot glass and jammed it into the burly man's flushing face.

A shriek that wasn't in the score came out of the clarinet. Someone in the booths screamed hysterically. A bar stool went over as someone else cringed away. Pops screamed. Then everything was whirling movement and yells, grabbing hands and hurtling shoulders, scrambles and sprawls, crashes and thumps, flashes of darkness and light, hot breaths and cold drafts, until Martin realized that he was running with Bobby beside him through gray pools of street light, around a corner into a darker street, around another corner...

Martin stopped dragging Bobby to a stop by her wrist. Her dress had fallen open. He could glimpse her small breasts. He grabbed her in his arms and buried his face in her warm neck, sucking in the sweet, heavy reek of gardenia.

She pulled away from him convulsively. "Come on, lover," she gasped in an agony of impatience. "Hurry, lover, hurry."

And they were running again. Another block and she led him up some hollowed steps and past a glass door and tarnished brass mailboxes and up a worn-carpeted stair. She fumbled at a door in a frenzy of haste, threw it open. He followed her into darkness.

"Oh, lover, hurry," she threw to him.

He slammed the door.

Then it came to him, and it stopped him in his tracks. The awful stench. There was gardenia in it, but that was the smallest part. It was an elaboration of all that is decayed and rotten in gardenia, swollen to an unbearable putrescence.

"Come to me, lover," he heard her cry. "Hurry, hurry, lover, hurry—what's the matter?"

The light went on. The room was small and dingy with table and chairs in the center and dark, overstuffed things back against the walls. Bobby dropped to the sagging sofa. Her face was white, taut, apprehensive.

"What did you say?" she asked him.

"That awful stink," he told her, involuntarily grimacing his distaste. "There must be something dead in here."

Suddenly her face turned to hate. "Get out!"

"Bobby," he pleaded, shocked. "Don't get angry. It's not your fault."

"Get out!"

"Bobby, what's the matter? Are you sick? You look green."

"*Get out!*"

"Bobby, what are you doing to your face? What's happening to you? *Bobby! BOBBY!*"

Pops spun the glass against the towel with practiced rhythm. He eyed the two girls on the opposite side of the bar with the fatherliness of an old and snub-nosed satyr. He drew out the moment as long as he could.

"Yep," he said finally, "it wasn't half an hour after he screwed the glass in that guy's face here that the police picked him up in the street outside her apartment, screaming and gibbering like a baboon. At first they were sure he was the one who killed her, and I guess they gave him a real going-over. But then it turned out he had an ironclad alibi for the time of the crime."

"Really?" the redhead asked.

Pops nodded. "Sure thing. Know who really did it? They found out."

"Who?" the cute little brunette prompted.

"The same guy that got the glass in his face," Pops announced triumphantly. "This Jeff Cooper fellow. Seems he was some sort of a racketeer. Got to know this Bobby in Michigan City. They had a fight up there, don't know what, guess maybe she was two-timing him. Anyway, she thought he was over being mad, and he let her think so. He brought her down to Chicago, took her to this apartment he had, and beat her to death."

"That's right," the old man affirmed, rubbing it in when the cute little brunette winced. "Beat her to death with a beer bottle."

The redhead inquired curiously, "Did she ever come here,

Pops? Did you ever see her?"

For a moment the glass in Pops' towel stopped twirling. Then he pursed his lips. "Nope," he said emphatically, "I couldn't have. 'Cause he murdered her the night he brought her down to Chicago. And that was a week before they found her." He chuckled. "A few days more and it would have been the sanitary inspectors who discovered the body—or the garbage man."

He leaned forward, smiling, waiting until the cute brunette had lifted her unwilling fascinated eyes. "Incidentally, that's why they couldn't pin it on this Martin Bellows kid. A week before—at the time she was killed—he was hundreds of miles away."

He twirled the gleaming glass. He noticed that the cute brunette was still intently watching him. "Yep," he said reflectively, "it was quite a job that other guy did on her. Beat her to death with a beer bottle. Broke the bottle doing it. One of the last swipes he gave her laid her face open all the way from her left temple to her right ear."

THE END

THE SISTERS

By Gordon Schendel

Do you remember a radio show—long gone—called "Lights Out"? And there was another eerie little job they named "The Hermit's Cave." Well, if you liked their brand of gleeful ghoulishness, you'll go for this yarn. 'Nough said.

THE big, ugly old house on the edge of town, half hidden by somber blue spruce, was set well back from the road in two acres of weed-grown lawn bounded by a rusting wrought-iron fence. Long ago, the house had been the town showplace and the scene of lavish parties and musicales, but now children walked quickly when they were forced to pass it and virtually no outsider ever entered its sagging scrolled gates.

Twilight was fast blurring the harsh outlines of the tortuous gingerbread fretwork, the shallow false balconies and the octagonal "tower" with its stained-glass windows. It was that stand-still time when the furry daylight creatures have retired and the creatures of darkness have not yet crept out of their holes from under their rotting logs or up through the green slime of stagnant pools. It was the time, too, when the funereal firs exude their spicy aroma most pungently, and the small sounds of living only emphasize the heavy transitional silence.

A warbler in a twisted cedar near the house spilled forth a burst of song that died on a sad, haunting note. And from a wind warped sycamore standing alone in a distant field came a faint, final answer.

But the two middle-aged, startlingly-alike women who were striding about at one side of the house, with five or six nondescript cats, paid no attention to bird songs. The sisters— drably garbed, large boned, with their lank hair drawn tightly back from their gaunt faces—instead stalked grimly back and forth, each with a stick in her hand, peering intently at the ground.

Ellen Brewster was watching them from the narrow, dark kitchen of the house, where she was washing up the dishes. Abruptly—just as she set the last soapy plate on the wooden drainboard and poured out the dishwater—one sister screamed hoarsely at a cat which had pounced on something in the grass. Then she forced the animal away with her stick and stooped to pick up a small object. The other sister hurried over eagerly to peer at it.

Ellen dumped a box of wormy oatmeal, which she wasn't going to cook no matter what *they* said, into the meager garbage and carried it outside, carefully keeping the tool shed between herself and her employers. As she scattered the garbage over the fence, the sisters' shrill voices came to her clearly. After listening a moment, she tiptoed into the shed, picked her way between the stacked boxes of trash and rubbed at the dust-grimed window at the front with the heel of her hand. Priscilla Colton was standing directly beneath the window, holding a dead sparrow.

There was the sound of an unseen car grinding noisily into the graveled driveway. Startled, the sisters raised their heads and stared with undisguised hostility until a green sedan emerged into their view and drew up before the house.

"Oh, just Dr. Potter," Priscilla shrugged. The look of fascination returned to her face as she bent, once more, over the horrible thing in her hand, while her sister crowded close for a final look. Then, with a regretful sigh, Priscilla replaced the foul bit of carrion in the weeds, as gently as if it were some cherished pet. One of the cats darted forward, but she forestalled it with a vicious swipe of her stick that sent the animal caterwauling into the thick woods behind the house.

Shaking her head exasperatedly, Ellen left the shed and returned to the kitchen.

Dr. Potter stepped briskly out of his car and reached for his small black satchel. A chubby, white-haired man who retained the smooth pink cheeks, the guileless eyes and the unquenchably cheerful manner of a Boy Scout, Dr. Potter had been called in some years earlier by the Colton girls' father for what proved to be that old gentleman's final illness. And he'd continued to call once a week ever since, having transferred his administrations to the girls' mother. He'd treated the taciturn, now-bedridden old lady with an amazing variety of pills, medicines and bedside joviaties. But he either did not know, or at least never had disclosed, the name of the malady from which she'd so long been suffering.

"Good evening!" the doctor called breathlessly, approaching at an eager trot. "And how is your mother this evening?"

"Poorly, Doctor, poorly." Priscilla, always the spokesman, gave her stock answer to the stock question. And both sisters, like dutiful children reluctantly leaving their play, moved slowly forward, with their cats tumbling about their legs.

By now, the fading light in the western sky had almost completely drained off beneath the horizon, and a bat flittering overhead was virtually invisible against the firs. Priscilla stepped onto the sagging porch and silently opened the front door. Dr. Potter moved past her with a "Thank you!" that sounded much too loud in the pitch-black, musty-smelling parlor.

In the distance, from across the flat farmlands that had once been marsh, a hound bayed eerily, and the doctor waited almost nervously for one of the sisters to strike a light. But the girls had spun around in the doorway to stare back into the night.

"Hear that hound howl?" Priscilla asked, tensely. "Somebody," she whispered hoarsely, "is going to die."

"Or *has* died," Delight chimed in. "I wonder who? Old man Harrigan...? Mrs. Feeley...?" Her voice was tremulous and avid, as though she were tantalizing herself with exciting guesses.

"Nonsense, girls, nonsense. Pure superstition!" the doctor interjected, testily.

The hound bayed again, and the rising night wind brought the mournful keening suddenly closer.

Priscilla emitted an almost ecstatic sigh.

Dr. Potter cleared his throat. "May we have a light, please?" His tone implied, tactfully but firmly, that his professional time was extremely valuable.

There was a moment of delay, as if the sisters were hoping for the hound to again give voice. Then Priscilla made her way swiftly into the dark room, the doctor heard the scrape of a match head on sandpaper and saw the tiny flare of light and Priscilla reaching overhead to light a gas jet on the wall. The flame shot up—almost every other house in town long since had been converted to electricity—and cast a weird pattern of light and shadow over the cavernous room, with its ornate Victorian furniture, stained and peeling wallpaper and painstakingly darned lace curtains that had been hanging at the tall, narrow windows nearly twenty years. The doctor wondered once more why the Coltons, with all their money, had let the place go to ruin so. But Priscilla was moving toward the open double doors of the adjoining downstairs bedroom and Dr. Potter, following, hastily resumed his professional smile.

Priscilla lit a gas jet just inside the doorway. Its feeble light revealed a massive carved bedstead piled high with rumpled patchwork quilts and, at its head, sunk deep in a goose down pillow, the face of Dr. Potter's elderly patient.

"Well, well," the doctor boomed cheerfully. "And how are you tonight, Mrs. Colton?"

There was no response from the bed—though usually the grim little old lady would open her beady eyes and scowl or mutter something unintelligible when thus aroused from her almost perpetual light naps.

Dr. Potter bent over the bed, jerked down the heavy quilts and placed his ear against his patient's wasted chest—at the same time picking up one of her bony, talon-like wrists. After a moment, he dropped her hand and quickly took his stethoscope from his little black bag, fitted the ear-plugs to his ears, and again bent over the old woman, applying the receiver cup to the region of her heart. After a minute he stood up, slowly, looking like an embarrassed small boy, about to cry.

"I'm sorry..." he said, in a sepulchral tone. "Your mother has passed away."

There was a stunned silence, as the girls looked unbelievingly from him to their mother. The dim light played grotesquely over the dead woman's deeply wrinkled, sunken cheeks, and sagging, toothless jaws. And, as the lamp flame flickered, it was reflected now and again by that part of the dead woman's eyeballs not covered by the drooped eyelids, giving the odd effect that the old lady was still slyly watching them.

"Poor Ma," Priscilla said mechanically. "She was just as always when I gave her her medicine."

But the sisters did not burst into tears. They stared at their dead mother silently and then back at the doctor, with a queer gleam in their eyes. Then they looked into each other's faces, tensely.

"When... How long ago?" Priscilla whispered, breathlessly.

The doctor cleared his throat.

"Not long," he said. To avoid looking into her piercing eyes, he turned to put his stethoscope back into his satchel, then gently pulled the sheet up over the face on the pillow. *"Rigor mortis* hasn't yet set in. Probably within the last hour."

In the silence that followed, the three who stood in the room once more heard the distant mournful baying of the hound.

The sisters' eyes met again, swiftly.

"It was Ma!" Priscilla gasped. "It was Ma that hound meant, and we didn't guess!"

"Girls, you can, er, be comforted by the thought that your mother is spared further suffering," the doctor said, uneasily. "She passed away peacefully."

He picked up his satchel and took a step toward the door. The sisters certainly showed little signs of grief, but after all they'd been expecting the old lady to die for years. Bedridden and senile, she'd only been half alive, anyway. Aloud, he said, briskly, "I'd better hurry back to town and phone Bartz before he goes to bed, so he can come out and get the body tonight yet," he was edging past the sisters, but abruptly Priscilla blocked his way, her eyes flashing wildly and her whole body trembling.

"No!...No!...No!" she almost shrieked. "We don't want the undertaker! He can't take our mother away! No! She belongs to us!...We'll never let him in!"

"But...But..." the doctor sputtered. "Now, now, Priscilla...I realize bereavement is always a shock. But you're a sensible woman. You know you can't keep your mother here."

"But we're *going* to keep her here! Aren't we, Delight?"

"Priscilla, please be sensible!" The doctor took out a handkerchief and patted his perspiring forehead. "Your mother's body *must* be embalmed and buried. Aside from the health regulations, you know you wouldn't want to keep it here. Besides," he floundered, "your mother already has left you; that's merely her body..."

Priscilla glared at him with a look of almost insane hatred. But after a moment, she dropped her eyes and capitulated, meekly. "All right, Doctor, just as you say. Bartz may come tonight. But he can't take her away with him. He must do his work here, where we can watch him! She's ours!"

"But..." Dr. Potter was aghast at what she was demanding. "Why, you don't want to witness that... Why..."

Priscilla's eyes flashed. "Yes, we do! Don't we, Delight?" Delight nodded agreement; her own eyes alight with anticipation. "He won't get inside this house otherwise! You tell him."

The doctor looked uncertainly from one grimly determined face to the other, then helplessly inclined his head to indicate he was accepting this gruesome compromise. He mumbled, "Good night!", and almost fled through the gloomy parlor. He turned at the front door to call back, sternly, "But for heaven's sake, keep those blasted cats out of your mother's room!"

Then Dr. Potter hurried through the dew-wet grass, climbed in his car, and jammed his foot down on the starter.

Henry Bartz was thinking how he hated his work as he drove his lumbering hearse on the road to the Colton place. He'd always been ashamed of making money from other folks' sorrow. And then, too, there was his wife's attitude: The day he'd completed his mortician's course after failing in the furniture business, she'd informed him she'd go into screaming hysterics if any hands that had messed around with dead people's bodies ever touched her own soft, voluptuous one. And though, during the years since, she'd proved to be not quite a woman with an unbreakable will, life had been difficult.

Bartz was driving the hearse rather than his car because he still hoped he could persuade the Colton sisters to allow him to take the body to his funeral parlor to do the embalming. But he doubted he'd have much luck. His thoughts shifted to the peculiarities of the Colton sisters.

Priscilla had been a born old maid from childhood. But Delight, the younger one, had been a popular, fun-loving girl, and in those days the big old mansion had been filled with a constant stream of her friends and admirers. The Coltons had gone abroad several times, and Delight had become engaged to the younger son of a titled family. But then, just before the wedding, her domineering mother and sister, who'd inexplicably opposed the match, had managed to break it up. Shortly thereafter, the young man had married an English girl—and Delight had changed overnight into a bitter carbon copy of her colorless older sister.

When old Jeremiah Colton had died, his wife and daughters had given him the most lavish funeral the town had ever known. And then they'd abruptly announced that there never would be another trip to Europe, that they would never again participate in the town's social life—and that they intended to have built, in the modest little hilltop cemetery, a $20,000 family mausoleum—a form of interment for the father so pretentious and foreign to the townspeople's concept of Christian burial that it was regarded as verging on the barbaric. And the Colton women had kept their word, for they never again had appeared in public except when they (infrequently) attended church, or a funeral (they never missed a funeral, whether or not they knew the deceased), or made their weekly pilgrimages to the big marble mausoleum to "visit" their father. And, though they spent large sums on floral pieces, and on their dismal excursions dressed in elegant black silk, they never again spent a cent on their home, or in entertaining, or in providing themselves with any of the comforts and little luxuries they could so well have afforded.

After their mother became bedridden, the girls almost never left the house. And little was known of their way of life, except from the tales of the disgruntled, low paid hired girls who came and went so rapidly—tales of the sisters' fantastic economies (the stale bread they bought because it was a couple of cents cheaper than the fresh, the grocers' crates they made the hired girls lug home to burn in the wood stove because they were free, the moldering furniture, the dangerous falling plaster, the unused upstairs bedrooms stacked halfway to the ceiling with boxes of trash, old newspapers and bottles); tales of the way the sisters allowed their numerous cats to run wild in the house; and, above all, of the sisters' morbid preoccupation with disease and death (their endless discussions of funerals and comparisons of one corpse with another, the medical and "doctor" books they avidly read, the little wakes they staged for the cats that died)…But though all of this was a frequent subject of gossip in the town, most people had a hard time believing it, for the highly-respected Coltons had been the town's leading family, and besides, on the rare occasions when the sisters *did* appear in public, they still made a fine, genteel appearance…

But there was no doubt about it, the two old maids were certainly queer. Henry Bartz shook his head and stepped on the brake so abruptly that his man of all work who'd been snoring on the seat beside him was thrown forward against the dashboard. Old Jake swore softly, and Bartz turned between the big sagging gates and into the poplar-lined driveway. The hearse bounced over the ruts, creaking and groaning, and came to a stop before the monstrous old house—a shapeless black mass in the moonlight, with light gleaming feebly through only a single side window.

Bartz tossed away his mangled cigar butt, strode onto the porch and knocked on the screen door. An owl hidden overhead in the dark spruces hooted weirdly. Then Bartz jumped, startled, as a voice spoke from the darkness not more than three feet away.

"You can just turn that hearse around and drive it right back, Mr. Bartz! You won't be needing it," the voice said, furiously. "You're not taking our mother one step out of this house!"

Bartz now dimly made out the faces of the two sisters just inside the screen door—where they'd evidently been waiting in the darkness.

"We have Mother all ready for you," Priscilla continued, more calmly. "You may bring in your equipment and get to work. If you don't care to do that, we'll get the undertaker from Eastport."

Well, after all, Bartz told himself, wearily, he'd expected this. He called to old Jake to carry his paraphernalia inside. And then he groped his way after the sisters through the unlit parlor to the bedroom doorway. There he received a shock.

The bedroom was lit only by half-a-dozen wax tapers, flickering in a row at the head of the bed. But instead of being entirely covered with a sheet, as the doctor had left it, the pathetically wasted, shrunken body of the little old lady was laid out nude on the bed.

"My sister and I have washed and prepared her for you," Priscilla said, efficiently. "Now just go ahead with your work and don't mind us. We'll sit here and watch."

And with that, she and Delight sat down in the two straight-back chairs which were lined up before the bed like first-row seats in a theater.

"But, Miss Colton," Bartz gasped. "You can't really mean... You don't realize what you're saying. You don't understand what... Some of the things I have to do..." For he was remembering his own reaction the first time he'd witnessed the ghoulish routine he had to go through. Such things as the insertion of the anal plug...the draining of blood from the body, and substitution of the preservative fluid...the puncturing of the abdomen to provide an escape for forming gas...the tacking down of the eye-lids, the sewing together of the lips... He'd been violently sick to his stomach, even though he'd been a student, forewarned of what he was to see... And this was their own mother!

"We know just what you have to do, don't we, Delight?" Priscilla said primly. Delight nodded agreement and pulled her chair forward a little. "We do not wish to leave our Mother alone. So begin, Mr. Bartz!" Priscilla ordered, with finality.

Bartz looked from one pair of hungrily staring eyes to the other, and then at the shriveled body on the bed, over which the wavering yellow candlelight was playing queer tricks. The owl out in the spruces hooted again, derisively...

Just then Jake slouched through the doorway, loaded down with equipment. His jaw sagged and he almost dropped his armload when he saw the two sisters settled down expectantly beside the bed.

Henry Bartz never forgot that job.

He was naturally not a talkative man. And like a doctor, he'd always considered it unethical to discuss his profession. But he couldn't refrain from telling his wife about the night's work at the Colton place—and how the sisters had hung over his shoulder through every step, so as not to miss a movement. And, of course, then it got all around town the next day.

And that was the principal reason the funeral was so well attended three days later. Plain curiosity. Because, actually, brusque old lady Colton had alienated all of her still-living friends years before.

The Rev. J. Carleton Jones, a massive, consciously handsome man with neatly waved iron-gray hair and a jaunty mustache, sat in his study pleasantly re-living his funeral sermon. He rather enjoyed funerals. For, at funerals, he orated with a pipe-organ tremolo and, pulling all stops, fairly wallowed in emotionalism until there wasn't a dry eye in sight. His oration today had been particularly masterful, even though—he frowned, slightly—it had failed to wring a single tear from the two principal, black-veiled mourners. And it had been a pity that the steady drizzle had prevented many from going to the cemetery service. But, still, there had been mountains of flowers (mostly provided by the bereaved daughters), and only once before in his life had he had the honor of consigning a departed parishioner to that magnificent mausoleum.

The Reverend frowned again, as a timid knock interrupted his musings. It was Ellen Brewster, the Coltons' hired girl, still in her black funeral attire.

"Reverend, I'm sorry to bother you..." Ellen twisted her purse handle, nervously. "But I wonder if you'd know of a new place for me? You see, I've quit working for the Coltons."

"Oh, indeed, Ellen?" The Reverend nodded, sympathetically. "Yes, I'm sure we can easily find you another situation."

"Now that the Missus is dead," Ellen hesitated. "I felt they really didn't need me, and..." She burst into tears. "...And, oh Reverend...I just couldn't *stand* it any more!"

Tom Blasky, some weeks later, lay stretched out on the broken down cot he'd hauled into the cemetery caretaker's tool house, listening to the rain drumming on the tin roof. The rain had interrupted him in the digging of a grave. He lifted the already half-emptied pint of bootleg to his lips and, in a series of rapid, adamsapple-moving swallows, reduced it to a quarter pint. Then he recorked the bottle, wiped his mouth with the back of his dirt-seamed hand, and coughed explosively.

He'd been working at the cemetery over 20 years, digging graves and mowing grass. Working there had never bothered him—until recently. He'd seen the Colton sisters probably hundreds of times, beginning way back when they'd come to supervise the building of that big vault, more than ten years ago. Then they—and their mother, too, until she took to her bed— used to come out every week and put flowers on their father's casket.

Tom reached for the bottle again, uncorked it, and lifted it to his lips.

But the way they'd been since the old lady died—it wasn't good. No, it wasn't good. For nearly a month, now, they'd been coming every day, going inside the vault and staying sometimes hours… And twice already, they'd made him do something terrible! And he didn't want to do it again. He'd had enough nightmares about it already… But this storm ought to keep them home today, anyway. He was just drifting off to sleep when he heard somebody shouting his name:

"Tom! Tom Blasky! Wake up!"

The Colton sisters were standing over him in glistening rain-coats and hats.

"Mr. Blasky, will you get up, please!" Priscilla ordered. "We want you to come with us into the vault."

Tom stumbled to his feet. No, no, he told himself, he didn't want to do that again. He started to mumble protests, but Priscilla curtly cut him off, and he found himself following her through the doorway. As he slouched outside, after the sisters, the driving rain beat hard on his face. It was getting dark early, and the looming trees scattered over the burying ground were bending and swaying in the wind. And then a near-blinding, gigantic flash of lightning bared, all at once, with sudden ghostly

141

and gleaming clarity, the hundreds of pale marble and granite tombstones. In the immediately following blackness, Tom, who was staggering blindly after the sisters, ran head-on into their seldom-used, 25-year-old Packard sedan, parked in front of the tool house.

In another blinding flash of lightning and deafening crash of thunder, they finally reached the massive, white-marble mausoleum. Priscilla unlocked the heavy bronze doors, and the sisters stepped quickly inside. Tom, though soaked to the skin, followed only very reluctantly. Priscilla lighted two large wax candles which stood, partially burned, in niches in the wall directly above the two coffins (and beside the two still-empty coffin ledges). Delight shut the bronze doors until they were only slightly ajar, and at once the wild storm outside was muted by the thick stone walls.

Tom stood as close to the doors as possible, swaying unsteadily. This is not good, not good, he told himself. They shouldn't make me do this. The sisters moved to the newer coffin.

"All right, Tom," Priscilla said, her eyes shining oddly in the flickering candlelight. "You know what to do. Take the lid off mother's casket, so we can examine her again."

Tom moved unenthusiastically forward, put his hands on the lid and then recoiled.

"Come, Tom," Priscilla said, sharply, like a teacher reprimanding a recalcitrant child. "Hurry! Lift the lid."

With a groan, Tom moved forward again and set to work.

Though he'd intended to keep his eyes averted, they were drawn, as if by a magnet, to the dead woman's face—which, though sunken, in the moving shadows of the flickering candlelight seemed so alive that he felt a chill running down his back. Priscilla and Delight bent over the satin-lined casket. After a couple of minutes of silence, Priscilla cried out, in a queer voice:

"Look, something is seeping from under her arm!"

At that moment the wind shifted and a cold gust of wind and rain shot between the doors, blowing out the candles and leaving them in total darkness…a darkness suddenly heavy with a sickeningly sweet smell…the smell of death… And in the blackness, Tom had the nightmare feeling that he had been hopelessly locked in the tomb with the two corpses, that he was in his own grave and slowly, horribly, suffocating to death.

As from a great distance, he heard Priscilla saying, calmly, "I have the matches." And a moment later she had re-lit the candles. "Shut the doors tight, Tom," she said, grimly.

Badly shaken, he did as she ordered.

The next day Tom Blasky went to the First National Bank and told its president, portly, white-haired John Winters, who was chairman of the board of directors of the cemetery association, that he was quitting his job. Winters questioned him as to the reason, and so the story of the Colton sisters' macabre practices came out. Winters immediately called in Dr. Potter and Henry Bartz, who also were directors of the cemetery board, and after some shaking of heads, they drafted a note to the Colton girls. The note merely said that the cemetery association, in order to comply with state and village health regulations, henceforth was compelled to prohibit the opening of any coffin after it had been interred or placed in a vault, except under court order.

And so Tom Blasky never saw the old maids again. Not alive, that is.

Ten days later, Jimmy Mason, a small boy who lived on the edge of town, raced home to his mother almost too excited to talk, after having daringly peered in a window of the old Colton mansion. Dr. Potter, who was also the county coroner, hurried out to the place with big Charlie Wheeler, the town marshal. They drove the starving cats out of the house, then cut the two sisters down. The girls had hanged themselves, side by side, from the stairway balustrade. They'd been dead, Dr. Potter estimated, three days.

The sisters had willed their entire estate to the cemetery association, for the enlargement and improvement of the grounds and the perpetual upkeep of all the graves in it. It took cleaning women nearly a month to sort and haul out the mountains of trash stored in the house.

In the bookcase containing the medical books, the cleaning women found three ledgers in which Priscilla had kept a running journal. These ledgers eventually made their way into the hands of Dr. Potter. He spent a week reading every word—then burned them in his fireplace.

Priscilla's journal had been an interminable thesis on death— a compilation of literately set-down facts gleaned from medical and undertaking textbooks, interlarded with the sisters' observations at funerals, their wild imaginings on the subject of death and dying, and the day-by-day gruesome details of their parents' last illnesses—becoming, toward the end, clearly the product of a demented mind. Priscilla's journal had concluded:

"Since the Cemetery Association has high-handedly barred us from further studies on the person of our dead mother, only one avenue of research remains open to us. Delight and I therefore choose to learn the ultimate facts of death—by personally experiencing it."

THE END

THE MIRROR OF CAGLIOSTRO

By Robert Arthur

*A master fantasist creates a world of abysmal evil and dark
dimensions…a world that can be entered…or left…*

London, 1910

The girl's eyes were open. Her face, which had been so
softly young, flushed with champagne and excitement, was a
thing of horror now. Twisted with shock, contorted with the
final spasm of life ejected from the body it had tenanted, her
face was a mask of terror, frozen so until the rigor of sudden
death should release its hold. Only then would her muscles
relax and death be allowed to wipe away the transformation he
had wrought.

Charles, Duke of Burchester, wiped his fingers delicately on a
silk handkerchief. For a moment, looking down at the girl,
Molly Blanchard, his eyes lighted with interest. Was it truly
possible that in death the eyes photographed, as he had been
told, the last object that sight registered?

He bent over the girl huddled on the crimson carpet of the
small private dining room of Chubb's Restaurant, and stared
into the blue eyes that seemed to start from the contorted face.
Then he sighed and straightened. It was, after all, a fairy tale. If
the story had been true, her dead eyes should have mirrored two
tiny, grinning skulls, one in each—for a skull had been the last
thing she had seen in life. *His* skull.

But the blue eyes were cold and blank. He had seen in them
reflection from one of the tapers that burned upon the table,
still set with snowy linen and silver dishes from which they had
dined.

He amended the thought. From which Molly had dined.
Dined as she, poor lovely creature from some obscure group of

actors, had never dined before. He had dined afterwards. She had dined upon food, but he had dined upon life.

He felt replete now. It was a pity he had not been able to restrain his impulse to kill. London was a city of infinite interest in this, the twentieth century. He should have planned on a prolonged stay, to explore it fully, but temptation had been too great, after so long an abstinence.

HE moved swiftly now. The cheap necklace of glass beads, which the girl's mind had seen as rare diamonds, he allowed to remain about the throat where they glistened against the blue marks of strangling fingers. But he took his cloak from a hook and threw it over his shoulders. He retrieved his hat and let himself out the door without a backward glance for the empty husk that lay upon the rug.

A waiter in red livery was coming down the hall, past the series of closed doors that led to the famous—and infamous—private dining rooms of Chubb's. Charles stopped him.

"I leave," he said. "My friend—" he nodded toward the closed door— "wishes to be undisturbed so that she may compose herself. Please see to it."

A coin slipped from one hand to the other, and the servitor nodded.

"Very good, Sir," he said. No titles and no names were used at Chubb's. They were, however, well known to both the proprietor and all the help. A pity.

Charles walked down the long corridor, down the steps which led to the street without imposing upon one the necessity of exposing himself to the view of the crowd in the dining rooms below. As he let himself out, the eight-foot tall doorman, cloaked in crimson with a black shakko upon his head—a sight more goggled at in these days by tourists from puritanical America than even Windsor Castle—raised a hand. A hansom cab arrived in place precisely on the moment that his steps carried him to the curb.

Without looking back, Charles tossed a coin over his shoulder. The giant doorman casually retrieved it from the air as a dozen beggars and street loungers leaped futilely for it.

"Burchester House," Charles said to the coachman.

He settled back to stare with hungry eyes upon this, the new London of which he had seen so little—and could have seen so much if he had not let himself be carried away by the soft sweet temptation of Molly Blanchard's life so that…

But it was futile to dwell upon it. There would be other occasions. As they rolled through the dark streets he let himself relive the moment when he had placed the necklace about Molly's throat, telling her to look deep into his eyes. The heady delight of the instant when her trusting eyes had seen behind the mask of flesh which he now wore. The almost intolerable joy of her struggles.

HE realized that the hansom had stopped. For how long had he been living again those delights, unaware? There was not, after all, infinity ahead of him yet. Pursuit would be hot after him soon, and he was as vulnerable now as a new-hatched chick.

He stepped from the cab and flung the driver money. Charles, still with the down of youth upon his pink and white cheeks, strolled with the gait of a man much older and more experienced into the great, three-storied stone mansion which was the London residence of the Burchesters.

Inside, someone came scurrying out of the shadows of the almost dark parlor.

"Charles, my son," his mother began, in a voice that trembled.

"Later, mother," he said sharply, and brushed past her. "I am going to my studio. I will be occupied for some time." He started up the stairs toward the tower room where he kept his paints and canvases. Behind him he heard his mother whimpering. He paid no heed. As he reached the second floor he increased his pace. It would not do to be late in getting back to his sanctuary.

An hour later, with his mother weeping outside his door and the men from Scotland Yard hammering on it, Charles, Duke of Burchester, flung himself from the casement window and jellied himself on the cobblestones below.

Paris, 1963

The Musée des Antiquités Historique was a small brick building, twisted out of shape by the pressure of time and its neighbors. It stood at the end of one of Paris' many obscure streets, so narrow and twisting that no driver of even the smallest car, entering one, could be sure of finding room enough to turn around to get out again.

Beyond the Musée flowed the Seine, and if the waters of the Seine gave off any glint of light this overcast day, the glint was wholly lost in passing through the grime that darkly frosted the windows of the office of the curator, Professor Henri Thibaut.

Thibaut himself was ancient enough to seem one of the museum's exhibits, rather than its curator. But his eyes still snapped, and he spoke with a swift crispness that strained Harry Langham's otherwise excellent understanding of French.

"Cagliostro?" Thibaut said, and the word seemed to uncoil from his lips like a tiny serpent of sound. "Count Alexander Cagliostro, self-styled. Born in 1743, died in 1795. A man of great controversy. By some denounced as a fraud. By others acclaimed as a miracle worker—a veritable magician. Ah yes, my young colleague from America, I have studied his life. Your information is entirely correct."

"Good," Harry Langham said. He smiled. At thirty-five he still seemed younger than his age, although a carefully acquired professorial manner helped counterbalance his youthful aspect.

"Frankly, sir," he added, "I had just about given up hope of getting any decent information about Cagliostro to make my summer in Europe worthwhile. I'm an associate professor of history at Boston College—my period is the 18th Century—and

I am working for my doctorate, you see. I have chosen Count Cagliostro as the subject for my thesis. This is my last day in France. Only last night I heard of you—heard that you yourself had once written a thesis on the life of Cagliostro. I'm here, hoping you will assist me."

"Ah." Thibaut took a cigarette from an ivory box and lit it. "And from what viewpoint do you approach your subject? Do you propose to expose him as one of history's great frauds? Or will you credit him with powers bordering on the magical?"

"That's my problem," Harry Langham said frankly. "To play it safe I ought to call him a mountebank, a faker, a great charlatan. But I can't. I started thinking that, and now—now I believe that he may really have had mystic powers. His life is wrapped in such mystery—"

"And you wish to clarify the mystery?" Thibaut said, his tone sardonic. "You will write your thesis about Cagliostro. You will win an advanced degree. You will get a promotion. You will make more salary. You will marry some attractive woman. All from the dusty remains of Cagliostro. N'est-ce pas?"

"Well—yes." Harry Langham laughed, a bit uneasily. "Cagliostro—thesis—promotion—money—marriage. Almost like an equation, isn't it?"

"It is indeed." With a sudden motion, Thibaut ground out his cigarette. "Except that the answer is wrong."

"How do you mean?"

"Cagliostro can bring you only grief. Go back to America and erase the name of Cagliostro from your memory."

"But Professor!" Harry reflected that the French became excited easily, and the thought made his tone amused. "You yourself wrote a thesis about the man."

"And destroyed it." Thibaut sank back into his chair. "Some things our world will not accept. The truth about Count Cagliostro is one of them."

"But he's been dead for nearly two hundred years!"

M'SIEU Langham," Thibaut said, reaching again for the cigarettes in the ivory box, "evil never dies. No, no. Do not answer. There is little I can do to help you. I destroyed my thesis and all my notes. "However, if you should go to London—"

"I go there tomorrow," Harry told him. "I sail from Southampton in a week. I hope to find some material on Cagliostro in the British Museum."

"You will find little of value," the Frenchman said. "To the British, Cagliostro was a charlatan. But attend. Seek in the old furniture shops for a plain desk with a hinged lid, the letter "C" carved into it in ornate scrolls. Once it belonged to Cagliostro. Later it was acquired by one of the Dukes of Burchester. I have reason to believe that certain of Cagliostro's papers were hidden in a secret drawer in this desk and may possibly still be there."

"A plain desk with a hinged lid, the letter "C" carved into it." Harry Langham's expression was eager. "That would be a find indeed. I certainly thank you, Professor Thibaut."

The older man eyed him sadly.

"I still repeat my advice—tear up your thesis, forget the name. But you are young, you will not do it. Very well, I shall make one more suggestion. Go—now, today—to the Church of St. Martin."

"St. Martin?"

"I will give you the address. Find the caretaker, give him ten new francs. Tell him you wish to see the tomb of Yvette Dulaine."

"Yvette Dulaine?"

"She was buried there in 1780."

"But I don't understand—I mean, what point is there in seeing the tomb of a girl who died in 1780?"

"I said she was buried then." Thibaut's gaze was inscrutable. "Insist that the caretaker open the tomb for you. Then do whatever you must do. Au revoir, my young friend."

IN the age-wracked Museum of Historic Antiquities, it had been easy to smile at the melodramatic earnestness of the French. Here, with the streets of Paris, Lord alone knew how many feet above his head, moving down a narrow stone passageway slippery with seepage of water, holding aloft his own candle and following the flickering flame borne by the rheumatic old man in front of him, Harry found it less easy to smile.

They had gone down endless steps, along corridors that turned a dozen times. How old was this church anyway, and how far into the bowels of the earth did its subterranean crypts go? The whole thing was too much like an old movie for Harry Langham's taste. Except that the smell of damp corruption in the air, the shuffle of the old man's shoes on the rock flooring, and the scamper of rats in the darkness carried their own conviction.

They passed another room opening off the corridor, a room into which the bobbing candle flames sent just enough light to show old, elaborately carved stone tombs in close-joined ranks.

"Is this it?" Harry asked impatiently, as his guide paused. "We must be there by now. We have had time enough to travel halfway across Paris."

"Patience, my son." The caretaker's tone was unhurried. "Those who lie here can not come to us. We must go to them."

"Then let's hurry it up. This is my last day in Paris. I have a thousand things to tend to."

They went on, around another turning, down some stairs and came into a low-ceilinged room dug from solid rock. The tombs here were simpler. Many had only a name and a date. In the light from the two candles, they lay like sleeping monsters of stone, jealously hiding within them the bones of the humans they had swallowed.

"Are we there at last?" Harry Langham's tone was ironic. "Thank heaven for that! Now which of these dandy little one-room apartments belongs to Miss Yvette Dulaine? I've come this far. I'll see it, but then I'm heading back for fresh air."

"None of these," the caretaker said quietly. "She lies over here, la pauvre petite. Come."

He skirted the outer row of tombs and paused, lifting his candle high. In a crude niche in the stone a tomb apart from the others had been placed. It could have been no plainer—stone sides, a stone slab on top, the date *1780* cut into the top, no other inscription.

"She is here. It is only the second time in this century that she has been disturbed."

HARRY stared skeptically at the simple tomb. His shoes were damp and he felt chilled as well as somehow disappointed.

"Well?" he asked. "What am I supposed to do? Say ooh and aah? Why isn't her name on it—just the date? How do I know this is even Yvette Dulaine's tomb?"

The caretaker straightened painfully. He held his candle up and stared into Harry's face.

"You are American," he said. "When this tomb was closed, your nation had but begun its destiny. You have much to learn."

"Look," Harry said, controlling his impatience with an effort. "I agree we have a lot to learn. But I can't see I'm learning much here, looking at some chunks of stone that hide a lady who died one hundred and eighty-odd years ago."

"Ah." The other spoke gently. "If she had but died."

"If she had but—" Harry stared at him. "What are you talking about? They don't bury you unless you're dead. Believe me, I know."

"M'sieu's knowledge is no doubt formidable." The other's tone was gentle, the sarcasm in his words. "Let us now disturb the peace of Mlle Dulaine for but one moment more. We shall open her tomb."

"Now really, that's hardly necessary—" Harry began, but stopped when the caretaker handed him his candle and grasped the bottom end of the slab top. He tugged; inch by inch the heavy stone moved, screeching its protest. Harry had no special desire to see some mouldering bones. He had avoided such a tourist attraction as the catacombs of Paris, just because he didn't care for morbid reminders of man's mortality. He liked his life—and death—in the pages of books. Both life and death were neat and tidy there and could be studied without emotion. He did not look into the open tomb until the caretaker straightened and motioned with his hand.

"Perceive," he said. "Look well upon the contents of this tomb, which the good fathers left nameless so that the poor one inside would not disturb the thoughts of the living."

Still holding the candles, Harry bent over. As he did so, the flames flickered wildly, as if buffeted by drafts from all sides, though no breath of air stirred there. And the shadows they created made the girl in the tomb seem to smile, as if she would open her eyes and speak.

Her face was madonna-like in its perfection of ivory beauty. Heavy black tresses, unbound, flowed down upon her breast. Her hands, small and exquisite, were crossed upon her bosom. She wore something white and simple which exposed her wrists and arms. As he bent over her Harry's hand shook and one of the candles dropped a blob of molten wax upon her wrist. He so completely expected her to move, to cry out at the pain, that when she did not he felt a sudden wild rage. At her, for seeming so alive, so beautiful and so desirable. At Thibaut for sending him here on a fool's errand. At the shriveled gnome of a caretaker for wasting his time on so childish a deception.

"Damn you!" he cried. "She's a wax figure! What kind of tomfoolery is this?"

WITH surprising strength, the caretaker thrust the stone lid back into place. Harry had one last glimpse of the young and lovely face with the lips that seemed about to speak, and then it was gone. And he could not explain why he felt doubly cheated, doubly angered.

"So!" he shouted. "You didn't want me to get another look! You knew I was going to touch her and see that she really was wax. Admit it and tell me why you bothered with this nonsense. Or is this a standard tourist attraction that you've rigged up to bring in a little income from gullible Americans?"

The Frenchman faced him with dignity, reaching for and taking back his candle.

"M'sieu," he said. "As I remarked, you are young, you have much to learn. Once, Mlle Dulaine attracted the attention of a certain Count Cagliostro. She refused him. He persisted. She rejected him utterly. One night she vanished from her home. The next day, servants of Count Cagliostro found her lying in his rooms, at the base of a great mirror as if she had been admiring herself. The Count was held blameless; he was far from Paris at the time.

"Mlle Dulaine seemed asleep, but did not waken. There was no mark on her. Yet she did not breathe and her heart did not beat. A week passed. A month. She remained unchanged. She did not begin that return to dust which is the fate of us all. So her sorrowing parents consigned her to the good fathers of the church, and they placed her here. She has remained as you see her, since the year 1780."

"That's idiotic," Harry said, shakily. "Such things aren't possible. She's a wax figure. She's certainly not dead."

"No, M'sieu. She is not dead. Yet she is not alive. She exists in some dark dimension it is not well to think of. The Count Cagliostro took his revenge upon her. She will sleep thus, until the very stones of Paris become dust around her. Now let us go. As you reminded me, you have many things to do."

"Wait a minute. I want to see that girl—that figure—again."

Harry's breathing was harsh in the silence; he felt his pulse pounding—with fury? With bafflement?—he couldn't tell what emotion he felt. But the caretaker was already moving toward the stairs.

In a moment he would be gone. Harry wanted to tear the stone slab off that tomb and satisfy himself. But to linger even a moment would mean to be lost in those stygian depths without a guide.

Furious, he followed the flickering candle that was already becoming small in the darkness.

IT was easy, in the daylight above, to regain his composure and laugh at himself for being tricked. It was easy, next day in London, when he met Bart Phillips, his closest friend at the university, who had spent the summer in London working toward his doctorate in chemistry, to entertain him with an elaborate account of the mummery he had gone through. It was easy to erase the lingering doubt that the girl had indeed been a wax figure.

Easy—until he found the mirror.

He found it in a dingy secondhand shop in Soho, called Bob's Odds and Ends. The desk he was seeking he had traced to an auction house which had suffered a fire. Presumably the desk had burned with many other rare pieces. But Bob's Odds and Ends had been mentioned in connection with the sale of the furnishings of Burchester House, residence of ducal line now extinct.

Bob himself, five feet tall and four feet around the waist, did not bother to remove the toothpick from between his unusually bad teeth when Harry, with Bart in protesting tow, asked about the desk.

"No, guvnor," the untidy fat man said. "No such article 'ere. Probably Murchison's got it, them wot'ad the fire."

"Come on, Harry," Bart said. "One last day in London and still you're dragging me to junk shops. Let's go get something to drink and see if we can't make a date with those girls from Charlestown we met."

"Don't 'urry off, gents," Bob said plaintively, unhooking fat thumbs from a greasy vest. "Got somethin' pretty near as good. 'Ow would you like to buy th' mirror wot killed th' Duke of Burchester 'imself?"

"Mirror?" Harry asked, the word tugging at his memory.

"Come on, Harry!" Bart exploded, but Harry was already following the fat man toward the dark recesses of the shop.

The mirror was a tall, oval pier glass, hinged so that it could be adjusted. It stood in a corner. As the fat man swung it out, it rolled on a sloping stretch of floor, toppled sideways, and would have crashed down upon him if he had not sidestepped nimbly. The mirror fell to the floor with a violence that should have sent flying glass for a dozen feet.

The proprietor looked at it calmly, then heaved it upright.

"That's 'ow it killed th' duke," he observed. "Fell on 'im. And 'im with an 'atchet in his 'and, like he was trying to smash it. But this glass can't smash. Unbreakable, it is."

"What's unbreakable?" Bart asked, following them.

"This mirror, according to the man," Harry said.

"Nonsense. Glass can't be made unbreakable," Bart said. "Good Lord, it's all painted over with black paint. It's no earthly use to anyone. Come on, I'm dying of thirst."

"But, gents, it's a rare mirror, it is," the fat man said sadly. "Without that paint, it'd be worth a pretty sum. Besides, it's an 'aunted mirror. It killed th' duke 'isself, and it stood in a closet for almost fifty years before that. Ever since th' duke's brother, wot was the duke then, murdered a girl in Chubb's Restaurant back in 1910, then jumped out th' window into th' courtyard an' broke his neck when the Bobbies came for 'im."

"Come on, Harry," Bart groaned. But Harry, on the verge of turning away, saw the faint glint of glass near the bottom where something sharp had scratched a few square inches of the black paint which covered the mirror's surface. It seemed to him the bit of glass reflected light, and he stooped to look into it.

He stared for a long minute, until Bart became alarmed and grabbed him by the shoulder.

"Harry!" he said. "My God, man, you're the color of putty. Are you sick?"

Harry Langham looked at him without seeing him.

"Bart," he said, "Bart—I saw a face in that mirror."

"Of course you did. Your own."

156

"No. I saw the face of that girl, Yvette Dulaine, who lies beneath St. Martin's Church in Paris. She was holding a candle, and looking out at me, and she tried to speak to me. I could read her lips. She said, 'Sauvez-moi!' Save me!"

WHAT in God's name has happened to Harry Langham?" Bart Phillips demanded, and ran his fingers through bristling red hair. "He's missed his classes two days in a row. Mrs. Graham, is he sick?"

The middle-aged woman, who might have stepped from one of the stiff portraits on the walls of the rundown Beacon Street house, compressed her lips.

"I don't know what has happened to him, Professor Phillips," she said. "He hasn't been himself for a week, not since he received word that mirror was due to be landed. Then since they delivered it two days ago he has not left his room. He makes me leave his meals outside the door. I have always considered Professor Langham a very fine lodger, but if this goes on—Well!"

She uttered the final exclamation to Bart Phillips' back as he took the broad, curving stairs of the once elegant house two at a time.

At the top, Bart hesitated outside Harry's door. Some dirty dishes sat on the floor just beside it. He tested the knob, found the door unlocked, and quietly pushed it open.

In the center of the big, old-fashioned room, Harry was on his knees before the oval pier glass, laboriously scraping away at the black paint which covered its surface. From time to time he paused to wet a rag in turpentine, rub down the surface he had scraped, and then begin again.

The younger man walked quietly up behind him. The glass, he saw, was now nearly free of obscuring paint. It shone with an unusual clarity, giving the effect of a great depth. Then Harry saw his reflection and leaped up.

"Bart!" he shouted. "What are you doing here? Why have you broken into my room?"

"Easy, boy, easy," Bart said, putting a hand on his shoulder. "What's the matter, are you in training for a nervous breakdown? I've been coming in your room without knocking for years."

"Yes—yes, of course." Harry Langham rubbed his forehead wearily. "Sorry, Bart. I'm edgy. Not enough sleep, I guess."

Bart looked at the flecks of paint on the floor, and rapped the mirror with his knuckle Harry started to protest, and subsided.

"At a guess," Bart said, "you have been working on this old looking glass since it got here. Now honestly, Harry, aren't you being—well, illogical? I mean, you think you saw a girl's face mysteriously looking out at you from this mirror, back in London. You've been on pins and needles ever since waiting for it to arrive—you've hardly been over to see us, and I must say that Sis is hurt, since she kind of got the idea you planned to propose. Tell me the truth—are you expecting that girl is going to appear in this mirror again? Is that what you've had all along in the back of your mind?"

"I don't know." Harry dropped into a chair and stared at himself in the mirror. "I tell you, Bart—I just don't know. I feel I *have* to get this mirror clean again. Then—well, I don't know what. But I have to get it clean."

"In other words, a neurotic compulsion," Bart told him. "Under an old church in Paris you saw a wax figure. Later your imagination played a trick on you—"

"It wasn't imagination!" Harry Langham leaped to his feet with a fury that astonished them both. "I saw her. I tell you I saw her!"

HE stopped, breathing harshly. His friend had fallen back a step in surprise.

"I—I'm sorry, Bart. Look, maybe I am being—unreasonable. Just let me get this mirror cleaned, and some sleep, and I'll be myself. And I'll come to dinner tomorrow night with you and Laura. How's that?"

"Well—all right." Bart said. "And you'll cover your classes Monday? I officially announced you had a virus, but I can't cover for you any more."

"I'll be at my classes. And thanks, Bart."

When Bart had left, Harry dropped into the chair again and stared at the gleaming mirror. It seemed to shine with a light which was not reflection, yet he could discover no source for it.

"Yvette," he said. "Yvette? Are you there? If you are—show yourself."

He knew he was acting ridiculously. Yet he did not care. He wanted to see her face again—the face he had seen in a tomb in Paris, the face he had seen in a bit of mirror in London, the face he saw in his dreams now.

Nothing happened. After a long moment, he got to work again with scraper, turpentine and steel wool.

The paint stuck doggedly. Twilight had dimmed the room to semi-darkness by the time the glass finally showed no trace of black remaining.

Exhausted, Harry sank back into his chair and stared at it. It was curious how brilliant a reflection it gave. Even in the twilight it showed every detail of his room. His studio couch, his bookshelves, his pictures, his hi-fi set—they seemed three dimensional.

He sighed with fatigue and his vision blurred. The reflection in the mirror clouded like wind-rippled water. He rubbed his eyes and once again the image was clear. The handsome black-and-white striped wallpaper, the crystal chandelier for candles, the old rosewood harpsichord, the enormous Oriental rug on the floor, the hunting-scene tapestry on one wall—

Harry Langham sat up abruptly. The room in the mirror was a place he had never seen in his life. It bore no more resemblance to his own room than—than—

And then she entered.

She wore something simple—he had never had an eye for clothes, he only knew it was elegant and expensive and of a style two centuries old. Her black hair was bound up in coiled tiers.

She carried a candle, and as she came toward him from one of the doorways that showed in the shadowy sides of the room, she paused to light the candelabra atop the harpsichord. Then she turned toward the man who was watching, his breathing quick and shallow, his pulse hammering. It was she. Yvette Dulaine, whose body lay buried beneath St. Martin's Church.

HE thought she was going to step into the room with him. But she stopped as if at an invisible barrier, and gave him a glance of infinite beseechment. Her lips moved. He could hear no sound, but he could read the words.

"Sauvez moi! M'sieu, je vous implorer. Sauvez-moi!"

"How?" he cried. "Tell me how?"

She made a gesture of helpless distress. A ripple swept across the mirror and she was gone. Harry Langham sprang to his feet.

"Come back!" he shouted. "Yvette, come back!"

Behind him the door opened. He turned in a fury, to see Mrs. Graham bearing a tray of food.

"What are you doing?" he shouted at her. "Why did you break in? You sent her away! You frightened her!"

The woman drew herself up in starchy dignity.

"I am not accustomed to being spoken to that way, Professor Langham," she said. "I knocked, and heard you say 'Come.' I have brought your dinner. I would prefer that you arrange to lodge elsewhere as soon as this month is up."

She set down the tray and marched like a grenadier out of the room.

Harry passed a hand hopelessly over his forehead. The sight of the food on the tray revolted him. He thrust it away and turned back to the mirror, which now was dull and lifeless in the almost darkened room.

"Yvette," he whispered. "Please. Please come back. Tell me how I can help you."

The mirror did not change. He flung himself into the chair and stared at it as if the very intensity of his willing would make it light again, would reveal the strange and elegant room it had shown before. The room darkened, until he could no longer see the mirror. Then his fingers, gripping the arms of the chair, relaxed. Exhaustion overcame his willpower, and he slept.

* * *

It was the booming of a clock that woke him. Or was it a voice, speaking insistently in his ear? Or a sound as of a thousand tinkling chimes intermingled? Or all three? He opened his eyes, and saw before him the mirror, light emanating from it. Once again it showed the strange room. The candles in the crystal chandelier glittered. And an elegantly dressed gentleman, who leaned against the harpsichord and watched, smiled.

"You are awake, m'sieu," he said, and now Harry heard the words clearly. "That is good. I have been waiting to speak to you."

Harry Langham rubbed his eyes, and sat up.

"Who are you?" he asked. "Where is she? Yvette, I mean."

"I am Count Lafontaine, at your service." The man bowed. "And Mademoiselle Dulaine will be here. She is waiting for you to join us. To save us."

"Save you?"

"We are both victims of an evil done long ago, before even your great-grandfather was born. The evil of the most evil of living men, Count Alexander Cagliostro. But with your help, that evil can be undone."

"How?" Harry demanded.

"In a moment I shall tell you. But here comes Mlle Dulaine. Will you not join us?"

Harry rose to his feet, feeling strangely light, disembodied.

"Join you?" he asked. And even as he spoke he was aware that his senses were dulled, his mind sleepy. "Is it possible?"

"Just step forward." The Count held out his hand. "I will assist you."

Beyond the man, Harry saw the girl come slowly into the room. She came toward him, slowly, on her face a look of infinite appeal.

"*Yvette,*" he cried. "Yvette!" He took two steps forward, and felt his hand grasped by the cold, inhuman fingers of the man within the mirror. The pull but assisted his unthinking impulse. For a moment he felt like a swimmer breasting icy water, shoulder deep. Then the sensation was gone and he was within the room in the mirror.

He looked with exultation into the eyes of the girl.

"Yvette," he said. "I'm here. I'm here to save you."

"Alas, m'sieu," she said. "Now you too have been trapped. Look."

He turned. The Count Lafontaine bowed to him, formally.

"A thousand thanks, my young friend," he said. "It is half a century since last I left the world of the mirror. I am hungry for the taste of life again—very hungry."

He kissed the tips of his fingers and flung the kiss to them.

"Adieu, mes enfants," he said. "Console each other in my absence."

HE strode confidently forward, and beyond him Harry saw, as through a window, his own room, dimly lit. The Frenchman stepped into the room and approached the chair where Harry had been seated, and now the shadowed figure in the chair, which he had not noticed before, was suddenly clear and vivid.

"*That's me,*" he gasped. "Yvette—that's me—asleep in the chair."

She stood beside him, her coiled dark hair coming to his shoulders, and infinite regret tinged her voice.

"Your body, M'sieu Langham. *You* are here, in the world of the mirror, this dark dimension which is not life and is not death and yet partakes of both. In your sleep he spoke the words of his spell and evoked your spirit forth from your body without your awareness. Now he will inhabit your body—for an hour, a day, a decade, I do not know."

"He?" Harry shook his head, fighting the sense of languor and oppression. "But who is he? He said—"

"He is the Count Alexander Cagliostro, M'sieu. And see— he lives again, in your body."

As they spoke, the figure that had emerged from the mirror world turned to smile at them with sardonic triumph. Then it settled down upon Harry's sleeping body, blended with it, vanished—and Harry saw himself rise, stretch and yawn and smile.

"Ah, it's good to be alive again, with a young body, a strong body." It was his voice speaking and in English—his voice, subtly accented.

"Now, au revoir. The night is still young."

"No!" Harry flung himself forward—and was stopped by an impalpable barrier. The glass of the mirror—yet it did not feel like glass. It felt like an icy net which for an instant yielded, then gathered resistance and threw him back. "You can't!" he cried. "Come back!"

"But I can," said Count Cagliostro reasonably, in Harry's own voice. "And I shall come back when it pleases me. Meanwhile, it is best that none save myself should be able to see you."

He raised his hand in the air and drew it downward, speaking a dozen words in rolling Latin. And Harry faced only darkness—an empty darkness that stretched beyond him, for an infinitude of time and space.

He lunged into it, and found himself spinning dizzily in a black void where there was neither substance nor direction. There was only a cube of light, from the mirror room, swiftly dwindling into a tiny gleam.

"Come back! You will be lost forever, M'sieu. I pray you, return!"

The words, faint and faraway, steadied his whirling senses. He saw the light, focused his thoughts on the room it represented, on the girl, and once more he stood beside her, with the candles flickering warmly above them and the hungry blackness behind him.

"Mon Dieu, I feared you were gone..." Her voice was unsteady. "M'sieu, we are alone here together. Even the consolation of death and the sweet sleep of eternity is denied us. At least, let us keep each other company and take what comfort we may from that."

"Yes, you're right." Harry passed a trembling hand over his face. "And maybe we'd better start with you telling me what in God's name has happened to us."

IT did not require many words, Harry thought dully, half stretched out upon a tapestried couch as he listened to the soft tone of Yvette's voice. She had rejected Cagliostro—and with a smile he had promised her that she would have all eternity in which to regret her decision. Then one night in her sleep a strange compulsion had taken her will, and she had gone to his home, admitted herself, and gone up to his empty room—to find him smiling at her from within the mirror. He had spoken— She had left her body behind crumpled on the floor and she had joined him in the world of the mirror. Then he—his own body many miles away—had left her alone there until the time came for him to take final refuge himself in the world between life and death of which the mirror was a door that he had opened.

"But he died in 1795 in prison," Harry protested.

"No, m'sieu. They but said he had died. His body is buried somewhere, as is mine, and like mine, it does not change. His spirit sought refuge here, in this sanctuary he planned long in advance. And from time to time he found means to escape, as he has now, in your body. Over the years, the crimes committed by various hands, yet all animated by the spirit of Cagliostro, would fill a library of horrors. One has heard of the Marquis de Sade. Yet the Marquis was but a man interested in things magical—until he encountered the mirror and met the gaze of Cagliostro. Then, m'sieu, the name of de Sade became synonymous with evil.

"Later, given but little choice, he assumed the flesh of a drunken servant who had entree only to the lowest of London's dives. It was then he acquired a nickname which you will know. Jacques."

"Jacques?"

"Jacques, the Ripper. Never was he caught, this Jacques. He froze to death in a gutter one winter night—but only after the spirit of Cagliostro had safely quitted his mortal flesh.

"And then young Charles, Duke of Burchester, acquired a desk and the mirror for his studio. And so fell into Cagliostro's power. But the evil Count was too greedy. The first night he killed a girl almost in public and must flee back to this, his place of safety. Charles, himself again, tried to break the mirror. When he could not, when the men of the police came for him, he covered the mirror with black paint, and then he threw himself from his window and was dashed to death on the stones below.

"Now, m'sieu—" her gaze was compassionate— "he is free again in your body. And the hunger is strong within him. I would speak words of consolation, but unfortunately I cannot."

"But what is he doing?" Harry started to his feet. "My God, Yvette, isn't there any way to know what he is up to and to stop him?"

"It is possible to know what he is doing," she said at last, "for the spirit still is connected with the body, though but faintly. But he can not be stopped. He is the master, we are his prisoners. And it is not wise to know what your body does at his orders."

"I must know. I have to know!" Harry declared feverishly.

"Then lie back, stare at the burning candles, and let your mind empty itself…"

HE was in a bar somewhere. A crowded, noisy, smoky dive. Impression of laughter, of voices. Of a face looking up into his. A hungry face, over-painted, yet still with some youthful sweetness in it not quite destroyed. They were moving. They were outdoors. They were strolling down a narrow street toward the waterfront, and light and sound here left behind.

The girl was petulant. She did not want to go. But he laughed, and with a hand on her elbow, urged her onward. They came to a railing, with the dark water swirling below, and a mist curling around them.

"No, I'll show you what I promised you," he was saying. "But first we must remove these."

He deftly removed from her ears the cheap, dangling crystal earrings, dropped them into his pocket.

"Why did you do that?" Her voice was shrill, angry. "You can't treat me like that."

"Your beauty should be unadorned. Look into my eyes."

She looked and her gaze grew fixed. In his eyes she saw the black void of eternity, and rising from it the grinning skull-face of Death. She did not struggle, did not scream as his hungry fingers closed around her throat. Only when it was too late did she fight, so deliciously, so rewardingly. When he dropped her over into the rolling waters below and saw them suck her down with hungry swiftness, he felt again deliciously warm and full...

"M'sieu! M'sieu!"

He opened his eyes. Yvette was shaking him, her face concerned.

"M'sieu, you looked so distressed! I told you it was not wise—"

"I'm a murderer," Harry groaned. "I killed her—killed that girl for the sheer lust of killing..."

"Comfort yourself, m'sieu. You did not. It was he, Cagliostro, slaking his hunger for life. It is thus his spirit feeds, grows strong—on the life of those he sacrifices."

"But it was my hands that choked her—Oh, my God, what are we going to do?"

He stood up, his hands clenched. "Can't we do *anything?*"

"Nothing, alas. He lives—in your body. We are shadows of the spirit trapped between life and death. Someday he will return and you will once more regain your body—"

"To be accused of all the infamous crimes he committed!" Harry cried. "To pay for them. But first, I'll break this mirror. That's one thing I won't fail to do."

Her gaze was wistful.

"If only that could be. Then I could at last die and be at rest. But you will not do what you think. Others have tried and failed. This mirror can not be broken by human hand—only he himself, Cagliostro, can break it. No—do not ask. I cannot answer how or why these things are. He has the knowledge. I have not. Now, you must distract yourself. Come—let me show you this world."

He let her take his hand, and numbly followed as she led.

THERE were doorways to the great room, several of them. She led him through one and he found himself in a small, booklined library, where alchemical apparatus crowded tables, and a small, white-globed lamp burned with a bright fierceness. A book lay open, revealing mystic symbols. A giant spider squatted upon it and stared at them with glistening pinpoint eyes.

"His library," Yvette said. "Once the mirror stood in this room in the world of reality. Everything the mirror reflected since it was made exists in this dark and fathomless dimension, if only it was reflected long enough; and his arts can call it into being."

"Like a time exposure being developed," Harry muttered to himself.

"Pardon?"

"I was just thinking. What lies beyond?"

"There are many rooms and a garden and even a pond. I will show you."

There were indeed other rooms, but Harry viewed them without interest. There was a garden where fruit trees bloomed, and a pool that reflected the sunlight of a sun not seen for two centuries. But when he would have gone on, through other doors, Yvette held him back.

"No, m'sieu. Beyond there is nothing. Darkness. Emptiness. Where one can become lost and wander until the end of time. And in the darkness there are—creatures."

She shivered as she spoke the word. But Harry persisted in his exploration. He opened a closed door—and there beyond it did indeed lie abysmal darkness. There were sounds in the darkness…flutings and wailings like no sounds he had ever heard before. And something darker than darkness itself drifted past as they watched, accompanied by the sound of a myriad of tiny bells. Swiftly Yvette slammed the door.

"Please, m'sieu," she panted. "Promise me. Never go into the darkness. Even Cagliostro knows not what it is or what creatures inhabit it."

"All right, Yvette." Harry agreed. "I promise. Let's go back. Maybe Cagliostro has returned. Maybe he'll be ready to give up my body now."

THEY returned through rooms of a dozen different sorts, one of them plainly the cabin of a ship. In the room of the mirror, the candles still burned as they had before, unconsumed and eternal. The wall of blackness which was the mirror remained in place. But even as they entered, it dissolved, became a window beyond which was Harry's study where Cagliostro sat at a table, eating breakfast and reading a newspaper.

He smiled smugly at them.

"I hope you have become well acquainted, mes enfants. I have waited for your return. M'sieu Langham, this body you have loaned me is a splendid one, so strong, so handsome, so indefatigable. I shall enjoy its use for a long time, I think. This time I make no foolish mistakes. I have begged the most humble pardon of Mrs. Graham, your good landlady, and she has forgiven me. This evening I dine with your friend, Bart, and his sister Laura, with whom I gather you have—what is the word?—an understanding. I must make amends to them for your behavior.

"Ah, my good friend, this Boston of yours is a most interesting city. Cold and reserved in appearance, yet it has its undercurrent of wickedness quite as naughty as London or Paris. I enjoyed myself last night. I was rash, perhaps, but fortunately I escaped detection. And now my motto is to be—discretion."

He rose and tossed down his napkin.

"Now, I shall rest," he said, and yawned. "Last night was—fatiguing. Tonight may be the same. Au 'voir."

He swept his hand downward with a roll of unknown words, and blackness sprang into place.

Wretchedly, Harry turned to the girl.

"How long were we?" he asked. "A dozen hours have passed since last night, but it seemed like only a few minutes—half an hour, perhaps."

"There is no time here," Yvette told him. "An hour may seem a day, a day an hour. You will become used to it, M'sieu Harry. Compose yourself—think not of Cagliostro."

She seated herself at the harpsichord and began to play a light, tinkling tune to which she sang in a sweet soprano. Harry flung himself down on the tapestried couch and listened. Gradually he relaxed. His mind ceased to throb and burn with turbulent thoughts. But as it did, other images, other sounds and sensations entered it.

Voices. Bart and Laura. Laughter. Wine.

* * *

"It's good to see you acting normal again, Harry. You had us worried."

"I don't wonder, old man. That mirror delusion—you brought me to my senses. Guess I worked too hard in Paris."

"Then there wasn't any girl in the mirror?" Laura's voice. Laura's smile. Laura's hand lightly on his arm as her eyes begged for assurance.

"If there was, she looked like me and needed a shave." Laughter. "Besides, what good would a girl in a mirror be?"

More laughter. "You'll see for yourself. When we set up housekeeping."

"Goodness. Is that a proposal? Or a proposition?" Wide, hopeful eyes, lips that hide a trembling eagerness.

"Look, you two—while you debate the question, I have to see a graduate student of mine who's working on an interesting line of experiment." Bart, rising, leaving. "I won't be back until late."

"Tactful Bart."

"A nice brother. I like him. Harry—"

"Yes?"

"Whether it was a proposal or a proposition, it's a little sudden. Since you got back from Europe, I've hardly seen you. Why, I think you've kissed me once."

"An oversight I plead guilty to. I can only say I'm prepared to make amends. Like this."

Warm lips. Tremulous response becoming breathless excitement.

"Harry! What *kind* of overwork did you do in Paris? What research were you engaged in, anyway?"

"Can not we go elsewhere...? This is better. My dear..."

Breathless excitement becoming recklessness.

"Harry! You mustn't!"

"Oh, yes, my dear I must."

"And I thought you were so prim and proper—even though I liked you."

"And I thought you the same. How wrong we can be about people? Now..."

* * *

"Stop!" Harry leaped to his feet, pressing his fists to his forehead, shutting out the damnable sensations from his distant body.

"M'sieu Harry." Yvette rose and came to him. Gently she touched his forehead. "It is Cagliostro again. You must not try to know what it is he does."

170

"I can't help it." Harry groaned. "My God, I never thought that Laura—"

"Do not speak of it. Shall I read to you? Shall we walk in the garden?"

"No, no... Yvette?"

"Yes?"

"Cagliostro controls whether or not we can see the world outside the mirror—and whether it can see us."

"That is true. He has charms that control it. If he speaks but the words, we can see and be seen but not heard. Or hear, but not be seen. And the greatest charm, that of drawing the spirit from the body and transporting it within the mirror. Alas, m'sieu, I crave your pardon."

"For what?"

"It was I—I who enticed you here. I could not help myself. Cagliostro worked magic that brought you to that shop in London where the mirror lay—he had waited long for the right moment. It was he who enabled you to see me. It was his doing that you determined you must own the mirror, must see me."

"I did feel—possessed," Harry admitted. "But don't blame yourself, Yvette. Even without Cagliostro you would have attracted me."

"You are gallant. I thank you."

"But what I started to say, if Cagliostro has charms, we can learn. We are not entirely helpless."

"Learn them? It is true, his books, his philters, his mystic objects are within his study—"

BUT in the study, where the white-globed lamp burned with an undying brilliance, Harry groaned and pushed away the strange books, the ancient parchments, after he had leafed through them.

"I can't read them. They're not Latin. Maybe Sanskrit. Maybe Sumerian. Maybe some language that died before history began."

"It is true," the girl told him. "Cagliostro has said that his magic is older than history, that it comes from a race so ancient no trace is left."

"And I don't believe in magic. That's one trouble. I belong to the twentieth century. Even here—even a victim of it—I still can't believe in *magic*."

"Oui," Yvette agreed, "belief is necessary. Without belief, the magic does not work. But then one must have faith in God, as well as in evil, m'sieu."

"Yes, of course." His eyes lighted. "And what is magic to one age is mere science to another. So why shouldn't science to one age be magic to another? Yvette, help me work this out."

"Anything I can do, anything," she said. "Sometimes Cagliostro had me help him. He said that in things mystic the female principal helps. Wait."

She took pins from her hair, let her tresses tumble down over her shoulder. From a drawer beneath the bookshelves she withdrew an odious object—the dried and shrunken head of a man who once had had flaming red hair and a red beard. She sat facing him, the head upon her lap.

"Now, m'sieu," she said. "This head—Cagliostro swore it was the head of one of the thieves crucified with the true Christ. Perhaps. But now I look like a sorceress. I will sit in silence, and you shall study."

"Good girl!" He plunged anew into an effort to make sense of the books, the cabalistic symbols. In his mind he thought of them as simply equations which produced certain results. So categorized, he was able to believe in them. After all, this mirror world—was it so much more than a photograph caught on celluloid, or a motion picture electronically impressed upon magnetic tape? Perhaps the people in pictures felt and thought...

And wasn't it Asimov, right here in Boston, who had said that some day the entire personality of a man could be put on tape, to remain forever, to be reproduced again whenever and as often as desired? What would existence inside a magnetized tape be? What thoughts would the man there think?

Perhaps his analogies were faulty, but they helped give him confidence. Yvette sat in silence as he worked, with feverish intensity. He deciphered a word, a sentence, for Cagliostro had translated into doggerel of Italian, French and Latin the older, unknown language—which might, after all, be the scientific language of a long dead race.

AS Yvette had said, there was no time in this place. At intervals he paused and put his fingers to throbbing temples. Then he was aware of sensations from the world of life. His classrooms. Students listening with rapt intensity they had never paid before. Himself speaking with brilliant detail of life in London, in Paris, in the 18th Century. A girl in the back row, blond, with a face as soft as a camellia. A girl who paused after class at his request.

"Miss Lee, you are very silent. Yet I think you are hiding a genuine intelligence. Are you afraid of me?"

"Afraid of you? Oh professor, I couldn't ever be that."

"You need confidence. You need—awareness. I would like to talk to you about yourself. Tonight?"

"Why—why, yes, professor."

…Night. His car. Driving. Lights. Stopping.

"Professor. What—what are you doing?"

"Look into my eyes, child. You are not afraid of me?"

"I—I—no, I trust you. I trust you forever and always."

"That is good. Now come."

HE forced his thoughts back to the books before him. He translated, worked out probable sequences, guessed where he had to. Still the awareness crept into his mind whenever he relaxed.

"Harry—I haven't seen you for so long."

"Working on my new thesis, Laura. That fraud Cagliostro—
I've torn him up. The new one is to be a comparison of social
life in London and Paris in the 18th Century."

"It sounds quite exciting."

"It will be masterly. But I must make up for my neglect. My
darling—"

"Harry! But—"

"No buts. Did you know that among the Romans—"

Doggedly he resumed work. But the outside impressions
pressed in more strongly.

An alley. Blare of music. A girl, provocative in a red dress.
She smiled into his eyes... And lay cold, moments later, in a
shadowed corner... Another girl. Walking home from a bus.
A scream. A struggle, sweet in its intensity...

"No," he groaned. "No, Yvette! The things he is doing!
The things *I* am doing! Even if I conquer him—I can't live.
Not with what I have done."

"Poor M'sieu Harry," she said. "But *can* you conquer him?
Suppose you force him to return here and give back your body,
what then? This mirror—it too is under a spell. It can be
broken only by Cagliostro."

"Maybe," Harry said grimly. "But it hasn't been tested in an
atomic explosion. In any case I'm pretty sure that, bathed in
hydrofluoric acid, it would dissolve. Or dropped into molten
glass it too would melt."

"But then—" Horror touched her features. "But then I
would be lost forever in the darkness that lies outside, lost
among the beings whose nature I know not. Only if the glass is
broken is the spell broken. Only then can spirit and body
reunite and blessedly find eternal sleep together."

"I see. But Cagliostro must be removed from the world. If
the mirror were dropped into the ocean where it is a mile deep."

She shuddered. But nodded.

"He must be removed, oui," she said. "What happens to
me—it is not important. Continue, m'sieu."

"I think I'm on the track." He pronounced some words, crudely. "Does that sound familiar?"

"Yes!" her face lighted. "It is what he speaks when he wishes to hear but not be seen. But it sounds like this—" She corrected his pronunciation. He repeated after her, the strange, rolling syllables.

"And this?" He spoke again, making a motion with his hand.

"When he wishes to see and be seen. Like this—" She corrected once more. "And his hands—I'm not sure—there is a certain movement…"

He tried, but did no better. Then he stiffened. They heard voices. Real voices. For the first time.

"Yvette!" he whispered. "We've won the first round. We can hear. Come, the other room. He is there, speaking to someone."

THEY moved swiftly back to the great room where one wall of seething darkness represented the mirror. And words came through it.

"Professor Langham?"

"Associate Professor only, I'm afraid."

"I'm Sergeant Burke, Homicide."

"So Mrs. Graham said. Homicide. Intriguing. What can I do for you, Sergeant?"

"Where were you at three this morning?"

"Here in my room. Working on my thesis. May I ask why you are interested?"

"A girl was strangled outside the Fishnet Bar last night."

"I don't believe I've heard of the place."

"One of your students was there. He believes he saw you with the girl who was killed."

"I am a very ordinary type, Sergeant. And one of my students—in a bar at three in the morning? No wonder they learn so little—academically speaking, of course."

"He described you pretty closely."

"Perhaps because he has seen me in class for weeks. Let me assure you, Sergeant, based on their class work, the powers of recognition and description of my students are limited."

"Maybe so. Do you know a girl named Elsie Lou Lee?"

"Of course. One of my students. A shy thing."

"She committed suicide last night. Cut her throat with a razor blade. Her last words were, 'He said he wished I was dead and out of the way, so I'm going to die!'"

"A suggestible type, may I remark?"

"Her landlady describes you as the man who sometimes called for her."

"Believe me, Sergeant, my description would fit twenty thousand men in Boston. I assure you I am too discreet to—fraternize—with a female student."

"Yeah, I suppose so. But frankly—well, we've had eight women killed in this city in four months. Eight! All young, all without motive. I have to check out everybody."

"Quite understandable."

"So—I haven't any warrant—but if you'd be willing to come down and make a statement at Headquarters…"

"With the greatest of pleasure. Let us go."

Footsteps. A door closing. Silence.

"If only we'd had the rest of the charm," Harry groaned. "So that the Sergeant could have seen us! Then we'd have had him for sure."

"He would have returned to the mirror," Yvette said sadly. "It is you who would have paid."

"Even so— Let's keep trying. Tell me again what he said and how he moved his hands."

Repetition. Endless. Timeless. Then abruptly the curtain of black vanished and they saw, through the window of the mirror, into his room. In time to see the door open and Laura enter.

She looked distraught and haggard. She advanced swiftly, calling in case Harry might be in the bedroom.

"Harry! Harry, are you here? I must talk to you!"

"Laura!" Harry cried. "Here. Here!"

She did not turn. She crossed the room, looked into the bedroom, then came and sat back on the studio couch, nervously pulling off her gloves.

"She does not hear," Yvette said. "There yet remains some part of the charm incorrect."

"*Laura,*" Harry groaned. "Please, for God's sake, look this way."

She did not immediately look toward the mirror. But as she sat, nervously playing with her gloves, her gaze swept the room—and finally stopped upon the mirror. And then she saw them.

Slowly, unbelievingly, she rose to her feet and approached them.

"Harry?" she whispered. "Harry?"

"Yes," he said, then realized she could not hear. He nodded instead. "Call the police!" He mouthed the words carefully but she stared at him with numb incomprehension. He turned to Yvette. "Quickly," he said. "Paper and pen."

Yvette ran. But before she returned, Harry saw himself enter the room. Cagliostro, as himself. And Laura, turning, stared from the man in the doorway to the image in the mirror with mounting disbelief and horror.

"Ah," said Cagliostro, approaching her. "Our friends have learned some tricks. I underestimated M'sieu Langham. Now you know."

"Know what?" Laura asked huskily. "Harry, I don't understand."

"You will, my dear. Alas. My plans were so well made. Marriage, a long and honorable career on the faculty. Unlimited opportunities to indulge my little hobby unsuspected—all professors seem so harmless. Now it must end. But perhaps there is still a chance—"

"Laura, look out!" Harry shouted, futilely, Cagliostro approached her—and then his hands were around her throat, throwing her back across the bed, controlling her struggles until she lay still. Breathing hard, he rose. He looked into the mirror.

"Blame yourself, M'sieu Langham," he said. "But then, I was growing tired of her. A possessive type. If I can but get her to the river, it is possible I may yet bluff your stupid police into believing in my innocence."

HE turned, and was drawing a blanket over Laura when the door burst open and Bart exploded into the room.

"Harry!" he shouted. "Where's Laura? Mrs. Graham said she came up here. My God, man, don't you know you were seen with that Lee girl only last night before she—"

Abruptly he was silent, staring at the still figure only half concealed.

"Laura fainted, Bart," Cagliostro said soothingly. "If you will go for a doctor—"

"Murderer!" The words were a strangled sob as Bart flung himself at the other man. Cagliostro stepped aside and Bart sprawled on the bed atop his sister's body. Before he recovered, Cagliostro held a needle-sharp paper knife he had snatched from the desk.

"My young friend," he said suavely, "usually I kill only women. But in your case I will make an exception."

With the litheness of a fencer he came forward, the point extended. But he was unacquainted with the game called football. The younger man lunged low, caught him around the knees, and flung him backwards. His body stopped only because it came into contact with the face of the mirror. And a myriad of cracks streaked the glass to its every corner.

"The glass!" Yvette said in fervent joy, as she and Harry saw Cagliostro crumple forward, with the paper knife still in his hand. "Cagliostro himself has broken it!"

Bart Phillips saw the cracked glass, and for just an instant he was aware of the two figures within the glass, figures already twisting and distorting as the glass came loose. A shower of a thousand sharp fragments fell across the prone man on the floor. In one fragment, Bart saw a single eye staring out at him. In another, a pair of lips murmured, "Merci."

Then the reflections were gone and the man on the floor groaned and with difficulty rolled over.

The paper knife emerged from his ribcage beside the heart, and dark blood stained his shirt and coat.

"Harry!" Bart dropped to his knee. "Harry, *why, why?*"

"I am not your doltish friend Harry, M'sieu," the dying man said. "He is lost in some strange dimension where there is neither light, nor time, nor space." His English now was accented. His features flowed, firmed. They became hook-nosed, sharp-jawed, the features of a man of middle age who has seen far too much of life.

"I am Count Alexander Cagliostro." The words came with difficulty and were punctuated with blood issuing from the mouth. "And I go now, his body mine, to meet the death which has awaited me patiently for almost two hundred years."

He fell back, limp, and in a space of seconds his skin became a loathsome corruption, his hair powdered, and the white bone showed through. The corruption became horror. The horror dried, became dust, and the very bones beneath it melted like wax, falling in upon themselves. A moment later and there were but fragments mixed with dust.

THE END

EACH MAN KILLS

By *Victoria Glad*

"...to live, you must feed on the living"

Now that it's all over, it seems like a bad dream. But when I look at Maria's picture on my desk, I realize it couldn't have been a dream. Actually, it was only six months ago that I sat at this same desk, looking at her picture, wondering what could have happened to her. It had been six weeks since there had been any word from her, and she had promised to write as soon as she arrived in Europe. Considering that my future rested in her small hands, I had every right to be apprehensive.

We had grown up together, had lost our folks within a few years of each other and had been fond of each other the way kids are apt to be. Then the change came: It seemed I loved her, and she was still just "fond" of me. During our early college days I sort of let things ride, but once we went on to graduate school, I began to crowd her.

The next thing I knew, she had signed up with a student tour destined for Central Europe, and told me she would give me my answer when she returned. I had to be content with that, but couldn't help worrying. Maria was a strange girl—withdrawn, dreamy and soft-hearted. Knowing the section she was going to, I was inclined to be uneasy, since it is the realm of gypsies, fortune tellers and the like. It is also the birthplace of many strange legends, and Maria claimed to be strongly psychic. As a matter of fact, she had foretold one or two things which were probably coincidental, like the death of our parents, and which even made an impression on me—and you'd hardly call me a "believer."

This so-called talent of hers led her into trouble on more than one occasion. I remember in her senior year at college she fell under the spell of a short, fat, greasy spook-reader with a strictly phony accent and all but gave her eye teeth away, until I realized something was amiss, got to the bottom of it, and dispatched friend spook-reader *pronto*. If she should meet some unscrupulous person now, with no one around to get her out of the scrape—but I didn't want to think of that. I was sure this time everything would be all right.

When she didn't write at first, I let it go that she was busy. Finally, six weeks' silent treatment aroused my curiosity. It also aroused my nasty temper, and the next thing I knew I was on a plane bound for the Continent. Within two hours after landing, I found her at a little inn in Transylvania, a quaint little place that looked as if it were made of gingerbread, and was surrounded by the huge, craggy Transylvania Mountain range. I also found Tod Hunter.

"What's wrong, Maria? Why didn't you write?" I asked.

Her usually gay, shining brown eyes flashed angrily. "Why couldn't you leave me alone? I told you not to come after me. I came here so I could think this out. For God's sake, Bill, can't you see I wanted to think? To be by myself?"

"But you promised to write," I persisted, wondering at this change in her, this impatience. Wondered, too, at her wraithlike slimness. She'd always been curved in the right places.

"Maria has been studying much too diligently," Tod said slowly. "She's always tired lately. She hasn't been too well, either. Her throat bothers her."

I wanted to punch his head in. For some reason I didn't like him. Not because I sensed his rivalry; I was above that. God knows I wanted her to be happy, above everything. It was just something about him that irritated me. An attitude. Not supercilious; I could have coped with that. Rather, it was a calm imperturbability that seemed to speak his faith in his eventual success, regardless of any effort on my part.

I don't know how to fight that sort of strategy. I look like I am: blunt and obvious. Suddenly I didn't care if he was there.

"Maria. Ria, darling. This guy's no good for you, can't you see that? What do you know about him?"

She looked at me, her eyes surprised and a little hurt. Then she looked at him, seemed to be looking *through* him and into herself, if you know what I mean. A slow flush spread from the base of her throat, that thin, almost transparent throat.

"All I have to know," she said softly. "I love him."

She looked out the window. "I'm going up into *Konigstein Mountain*, to a small sanitarium for my health shortly; the doctor has told me I must go away, and Tod has suggested this place. There Tod and I shall be married."

I knew then how it felt to be on the receiving end of a monkey-punch. That she had come to this decision because of my objections, I had not the slightest doubt. She was going to marry someone about whom she knew absolutely nothing. She was much more ill than she knew. Hunter was undoubtedly after her money; she was considerably well-off. Obviously she was once more being influenced in the wrong direction.

"I won't let you!" I warned. "Give it some more time, if for nothing else, then for old times' sake."

"How about me, Morris?" Tod interrupted. "You haven't asked me my feelings on the subject. I happen to love Maria dearly. Have I no say just because you're a childhood friend of hers?"

"Childhood friend! I was her whole family for years before she ever heard of you! I'll see you in hell before I let her marry you!" I shouted. Looking back, I'm sure that had he said anything else, I would have killed him, if Ria hadn't come between us.

"That's enough, Bill Morris! I've heard all I want to from you. I'm twenty-three, and if I choose to marry Tod, I'll do so and there's nothing you can do about it. Now, please go."

"Okay, Ria," I said, "if that's the way you want it. But I'm not through. If you won't protect yourself, I'll do it for you. I'd like to know more about the mysterious Mr. Tod Hunter, American, and I do wish, for your own sake, you'd do the same.

I wouldn't care if you married King Tut, so long as you knew all about him. People just don't marry strangers; not if they're smart. For God's sake, ask him about himself!"

"All right, Bill," she replied, smiling patiently. "I'll ask him. Now, do stop being childish."

"Okay, darling," I said sheepishly. "But do me one more favor. Don't marry him until I get back. Only a little while; give me a week. Just wait a little longer."

As I closed the door, I could still feel his smile, mocking— yet a little sad.

But Maria didn't wait. I was gone a week. I had walked my legs off trying to track down the elusive Mister Hunter and discovered exactly—nothing. All his landlady could tell me was that he was an American who had come to this climate for his health, and that he slept late mornings. I was licked and I knew it. If I had been a pup, I would have fitted my tail neatly between my legs and made for home. But I wasn't a pup, so I headed straight for Ria's flat to face the music.

They were waiting for me, she and Tod. When I saw her, I wished I were dead.

She lay in Tod's arms, her body a mere whisper of a body. White and cold she was, like frozen milk on a cold winter's day. They were both dead.

You know how it is when at a wake someone views the deceased and says kindly, "She's beautiful," and "she" isn't beautiful at all; just a made-up, lifeless handful of clay. Dead as dead, and frightening. Well, it wasn't that way this time. Their fair skins were faintly pink-tinted and their blonde heads, hers ashen and his a reddish cast, gleamed brightly. And they sat so close in the sofa before the fire, his head resting in the hollow of her throat. They looked—peaceful; no line marred their faces. I almost fancied I saw them breathe. And on her third finger, left hand, was the ring—a thin, platinum band. He had won, and in winning somehow he had lost. How they had died and why they found each other and death at the same time, I would probably never know. I only knew one thing: I had to get away from there—quickly. I almost ran the distance to my flat. Stumbled into the place and poured a triple Scotch which I could scarcely hold. The Scotch seared my throat and tasted bitter; someone must have poured salt in it. Then I realized that it was tears—my tears. I, Bill Morris, who hadn't cried since my fifth birthday—I was sobbing like a baby.

I didn't call the police. That would mean I would have to go back and watch them cover that lovely body, carry it away and submit it to untold indignities in order to ascertain the cause of death. The cleaning girl would find them in the morning and would notify the police.

But it wasn't so simple as that. In the morning I found I couldn't shake off the guilt which possessed me. Even two bottles of Scotch hadn't helped me to forget. I was dead drunk and cold sober at the same time.

I phoned Ria's landlady and told her I had failed to reach the Hunters by phone, that I was sure something was amiss. Would she please go to their flat and see if anything was wrong.

She was amused. "Really, Mr. Morris, you must be mistaken. Miss Maria went out just an hour ago with her new husband. Surely you are jesting. Why she has never looked better. So happy. They have left for *Konigstein*. They have also left you a note.

I told her I would be right over, and hopped a cab. I began to think I was losing my mind. I had seen them both—dead. The landlady had seen them this morning—*alive!*

When I arrived, the landlady looked at me for a long moment, taking in my rough, dark-blue complexion, unpressed clothes, red-rimmed eyes, then wagged a finger playfully.

"You are playing a joke, no? A wedding joke, maybe. Here, too, we haze newlyweds. But of course I understood. Who could help loving Miss Maria? Be of good heart, young man. For you there will be another, some day. But I talk too much. Here is your letter."

I went where I would be undisturbed, to the reading room of the library on the same street as my flat. To the musty, oblong, dimly lit room whose threshold sunshine and fresh air dared not cross. Without the saving warmth of sunlight or the fresh, clean relief of sweet-smelling air, I read. Read, inhaling the pungent, sour smell of the Scotch I had consumed during the long, sleepless night. Read, and then doubted that I had read at all—but the blue ink on the white paper forced me to acknowledge its actuality. It had been written by Hunter, in a neat, scholar's script.

Dear Morris: (It began)

Why should I not have wanted Maria? You did; others doubtless did. Why then should she not be mine? There are many things worse than being married to me; she might have married a man who beat her!

With her I have known the two happiest days of my life. I want no more than that. I have no right to ask for more. Have we, any of us, a right to endless bliss on this earth? Hardly.

You thought of her welfare above all; for that I owe you some explanation. You must be patient, you must believe, and in the end, you must do as I ask. You must.

You wanted to know about me—of my life before Maria. Before Maria? It seems strange to think about it. There is no life without Maria. Still, there was a time when for me she didn't exist. I have been constantly going forward to the day when I would meet her, yet there was a time when I didn't know where I would find her, or even what her name would be!

It was chance that brought us together. For me, good chance; for you, possibly ill chance; for Maria? Only she can say. Some three years ago I was studying in England under a Rhodes Scholarship. The future held great things for me. I was a Yank like yourself, and damn proud of it. Life in England seemed strange and slow and sometimes utterly dismal under Austerity. Then, little by little I slipped into their slower ways, growing to love the people for their spunk, and finally coming to feel I was one of them, so to speak.

I have said everything slowed down: I was wrong. Studying intensified for me. The folklore of the British Isles intrigued me. I delved into the Black Welsh tales, the mischievous fancies of the Irish, the English legends of the prowling werewolf. For me it was a relief from political science, which suddenly palled and which smacked of treason in the light of current events. My extracurricular research consumed the better part of my evenings. My books were and always have been a part of me, and as was to be expected, I overdid it. I studied too hard with too little let-up. Sometimes it seemed to me there was more truth to what I read than myth. It became somewhat of an obsession. Suddenly, one night, everything blacked out.

I came to in a sanatorium. I didn't know how I got there, and when they explained it to me, I laughed. I thought they were joking. When I tried to get up, to walk, I collapsed. Then I knew how bad it had been. I knew, too, I would have to go slowly.

It was there I met Eve. She was beautiful. Not like Maria, who is like a fragile, fair, spun-sugar angel. Eve was more earthy, with skin like ivory, creamy and rich and pale. Her blue-black hair she wore long and gathered in the back. She looked about twenty-five, but a streak of pure white ran back from each of her temples. She was the most striking woman I have ever met. I had never known anyone like her, nor have I since I saw her last.

You know how it is: the air of mystery about a woman makes a man like a kid again. She reminded me of a sleek, black cat, with her large, hazel eyes. I bumped into her one day on the verandah, and spent every day with her after that.

The doctors wanted me to take exercise—short walks and the like, and Eve went with me, struggling to keep up with me. The slightest effort tired her. She suffered from a rather nasty case of anemia. She seldom smiled; the effort was probably too much for her. I saw her really smile only once.

We had been on one of our short hikes in the woods close by the grounds. She stumbled over a twig or a branch, I'm not sure which. Suddenly she was in my arms. Have you ever held a cloud in your arms, Morris? So light she was, although she was almost as tall as I. Warm and pulsating. Her eyes held mine; it was almost uncanny. I have never been affected like that by a woman. Then I was kissing her; then a sharp sting, and I winced. There was the warm, salt taste of blood on my lips. I never knew how it happened. But she was smiling, her full mouth parted in the strangest smile I have ever seen. And those small white teeth gleamed; and in her eyes, which were all black pupils now, with the iris quite hidden, was desire—or something beyond desire. I couldn't define it then; now, I think I can. Her small, pink tongue darted over her lips, tasting, seeming to savor.

I was frightened, for some indefinable reason. I wanted to get away from her, from the woods, from myself. I grasped her arm roughly and we started back for the grounds. We never mentioned the episode again, but we neither of us ever forgot. She intrigued me now, more than ever. The doctors were able to satisfy my curiosity somewhat. They told me she had been a patient for some four years. Some days she was better, some days worse. She needed rest—much rest. Most days she slept past noon with their approval. Some days there was a faint flush beneath that ivory skin; other days it was pale and cool.

Just when we became lovers, I scarcely remember. Things were happening so fast I could barely keep pace with them. There was a magnetism about Eve which compelled. I couldn't have resisted if I'd wanted to—and I didn't.

I began to have long periods of lassitude, times when I would black out and remember nothing afterwards. And the dreams began. I would dream I was stroking a large, velvety-black cat, a cat with shining yellow eyes that looked at me as if they knew my every thought. I would stroke it continuously and it would nip me playfully. Then, one night the dream intensified: I was playing with the creature, caressing it gently, when of a sudden its lips drew back in a snarl, and without warning it sprang at my throat and buried its fangs deep! I thought I could feel life being drawn from me; I screamed.

The doctors told me afterwards that I was semi-conscious for days; that I had to be restrained.

When I was well again, Eve came to see me. She was gentle—soothing. She held me close to her and oh! it was good to be alive and to belong to someone.

I remember to this day what she wore. Black velvet lounging slacks, a low-necked amber satin blouse, caught at the "V" by a curiously wrought antique silver pin. It was round, about four inches in diameter. In its center was the carved figure of a serpent coiled to strike. Its eyes were deep amber topazes and its darting tongue was raised and set with a blood-red ruby.

"What an unusual pin, Eve," I said. "I've never seen it before, have I?"

"No," she replied. "It belongs to the deep, dark, seldom discussed skeleton in the Orcaczy closet, Tod. You see, my great-great grandmother was quite a wicked lady, to hear tell. Went in for Witches' masses and the like. They say she poisoned her husband, a rather elderly and very childish man, for her lover, whom she subsequently married. Together they did away with relatives who stood in the way of their accumulating more money. This pin was the instrument of death."

Her slim fingers pressed the ruby tongue and the pin opened, revealing a space large enough to secrete powder.

"It's like those employed by the infamous Borgias, as you can see," she continued, shrugging. "Perhaps it was fate then, that her devoted new husband tired of her once her fortune was assured him, took a young mistress for himself, and disposed of the unfortunate wife, using her own pin to perpetrate her murder. She was excommunicated by her church, too, which must have made it most unpleasant for her, poor old dear." The slim shoulders straightened. "But let's not discuss such unpleasant things, my dear. The important thing now is for you to get well quickly. I've missed you terribly, you know."

It was then I asked her to marry me. I knew I didn't really love her, but there seemed nothing to prevent our marriage. And she had gotten under my skin. It was as elemental as that. She said she thought we should wait until I fully recovered.

"Don't say any more, darling," she said. "Rest your poor, sore throat."

She bent over me solicitously and I reached up to stroke that smooth black hair. It had a familiar feel to it that I couldn't quite place. Of course I had stroked it hundreds of times before, but it wasn't that. Then she looked straight at me, those large, glowing hazel eyes boring into mine, and I knew. Knew and disbelieved at the same time. I froze where I lay, paralyzed by my fear; unable to make a sound.

"So you know," she whispered. "It is well. I have marked you for my own these many months. Now that you know, you will not fight. You know what I am, or at least you can guess. This pin you admired so—it was mine three hundred years ago and it will always be mine!"

Her lips were on mine. She had never kissed me like this. It was like the touch of hot ice, freezing, then searing. Unendurable. I lay inert; I couldn't have moved if I wanted to. I could scarcely breathe. Then I felt the blood within me pounding, pulsing, beginning to answer in spite of myself. I tasted once more the warm, salty fluid on my lips. Eve's body was liquid in my arms; warm, heady, narcotizing. Once again I felt the agonizing, dagger sharp pain in my throat and—darkness.

Have you ever wakened to a bright, sunny afternoon and heard yourself pronounced dead? They spoke in low, hushed tones. How unfortunate. Young fellow only thirty, dying so far away from his homeland. No family. Good thing he was well-set in life. This sudden anemia was most extraordinary; fellow showed no signs of it previously. All he had really needed was rest. If he had recovered, that lovely Eve Orcaczy might have made both their lives happier, richer. Sad ending to what might have been an idyll. Good of her to claim the body. She said she was going to inter it in the family vault in Konigstein Mountain *in Transylvania.*

I heard them distinctly. I wanted to shout that I wasn't dead; I wanted to wake up from this horrible nightmare. I was as alive as they. I knew I had to get out of there, some way; to get away from Eve, whom I now feared. They left to make arrangements.

The lassitude crept through me without warning; I dozed in spite of myself. And I dreamed again. I was a cat running, leaping through windows, loping over the countryside, stopping for no one. I panted with my exertions. Towns and cities flew by; I had to get someplace and quickly. Then the dream ended.

"Tod," she said, "Get up, my dear." I heard Her and I hated Her. Hated Her while I was drawn to Her. There was a white mist before my eyes. I reached up to brush it away. It was not a mist; it was a cloth. I shivered.

"I must wake up," I whispered hoarsely. "I must! I'm going mad!"

There was a creaking sound and daylight descended upon me. When I saw where I was, I covered my face with my hands and sobbed. I tried to pray, but the words froze on my lips. I was sitting in a coffin in a mausoleum! I had been buried alive!

"What am I?" I shrieked. "Where am I and what have You done? I'm out of my mind; stark, staring mad!"

Eve's lips parted, showing the even white teeth—those slightly pointed teeth.

"You're quite sane, my dear," She said calmly. "You are now one of us; a revenant, even as I, and to live you must feed on the living."

"It's not true!" I shouted. "This is all a crazy nightmare, part of my illness! You're not real! Nothing is real!"

"I'm quite real, Tod. To be trite, I am what I am, and have accepted it calmly, as you shall in time. I have told you of my life. You have been a student of legends. Legends are often—more often than you think—reality. When one has been murdered, if one has lived a so-called wicked life, he is doomed to walk the earth battening on the living. My fate was sealed as I lay in my coffin. But that wasn't enough. As I lay there, my pet cat, Suma, slunk into the room and leapt over me. That was a double insurance of my life after death. Those whom I mark for my own must, too, live on. Accept it, my dear. You have no other choice."

"No!" I cried. "I'm an American! Things like this don't happen to us! It's only in stories, and then to foreigners!"

She chuckled drily. "I'm afraid these things do happen, and in this case, you're it, my dear. Make the best of it."

But I wouldn't; I refused to—for a while. I would not feast on the blood of the living. Something within me fought. For a time.

Then, the awful hunger began. The tearing pangs of hunger that ordinary food wouldn't arrest. I fought it as long as I could. I lost.

First it was small animals; animals that I loved. It was my life or theirs. Then there was a little girl; a dear little creature who might have been my child under different circumstances.

After the episode of the little girl, Eve left me. She had no further use for me; she had wanted the child, too, and I had got it. I was now competition to be shunned. I was alone once again, alone and thoroughly miserable. I couldn't understand myself, my motives, so how could I expect someone else to understand?

I only knew what I was; I could not rationalize on why I had become this way. I could only presume it had happened to others equally as innocent as myself of wrong-doing. In the daytime, when I was like others, I reproached myself; goodness knows I loathed myself and what I had to do in order to "live." I wished I might really die, for I was tired—so frightfully tired and sick of it all. But I knew of no way to accomplish this, so I had to bear it all, fasting until my voracious, disgusting appetites got the better of me.

I decided there must be some information on my kind, particularly in this area where vampire legends are rife, so I took to haunting reading rooms. It was there I met Maria. She told me, after we knew each other better, that she was doing graduate work in regional superstitions and had decided that her thesis would treat of the history of vampirism. She found it terribly amusing, but at the same time frightening: Didn't I? I fear I saw nothing laughable about it, but I held my peace. Why, I could have done a thesis for her that would have driven some mild-mannered prof completely out of his mind! I kept my knowledge to myself, though; I didn't want to scare Maria.

She was like a flash of sunshine in a darkened room. She made each day worth living. For the first time the hunger pangs ceased. Ceased for one week, then two. I was certain I was cured. Perhaps, I thought, the whole thing was just a dream and I am finally awake.

I felt then I had the right to tell her of my love. She looked infinitely sad. She wasn't certain, she said. She knew she was awfully fond of me, but she was confused. She had just come away from the States, trying to make up her mind about someone dear, whom she didn't want to hurt, and she wanted a breather. I said I would wait up to and through eternity, if she wished.

Things went along peacefully then. We would walk for hours together, walk in complete silence and understanding. My strength seemed to be returning more day by day. We went far afield in search of material for her thesis. She would track down the most minute speck of hearsay, to get authenticity.

One day, in our wanderings, I thoughtlessly let myself be led too near my resting place. One of the locals mentioned a "place of horror" nearby and Maria wanted to investigate. I had no choice. We poked amid the still fustiness of the deserted mausoleum I knew so well. She thought it odd that the door was unlocked. I said, yes, wasn't it. Then she saw the box, that gleaming copper box which Eve had so thoughtfully provided. She stroked it gently, commenting on its beauty, and before I could prevent it or divert her attention, she had lifted the heavy lid exposing the disarranged shroud, the remains of one or two hapless small creatures, the horrible blood-stained satin lining. She screamed and dropped the lid, somehow pinching her finger. She hopped on one foot, as one usually does to fight down sudden pain. Then she was clinging to me, thoroughly frightened.

"What does it mean, Tod?"

I quieted her with the usual platitudes. Then I was kissing that poor, red little finger. Without warning to myself or her, I nipped it affectionately. A warm glow spread through me; there was a taste more delightful than fine old brandy, or vintage wine, and I knew irrevocably that I was not cured; no, nor ever should be! And I knew, too, that I wanted Maria—not just as a man longs for the woman he loves—but to drink of the fountain of her life, that warm, intoxicating fountain, greedily, joyously. She never knew what went through my mind at that moment. If I could have killed myself then, I would have, and with no compunction. But there is more to killing a revenant than that. The Church knows the procedure. I hurried Maria home as fast as I could and told her I had to go away for a week on business. She believed me and said she would miss me. But I didn't go away. That night I fought a losing battle with myself, and then and every night thereafter, I returned to her, partook of her and slunk away, loathing myself. I knew that I must soon kill the one being I loved above all others, kill, too, her immortal soul, and there was nothing I could do to prevent it.

She began to fade visibly. When I "returned" in a week, she was so ill that a few steps tired her. Her appetite all but vanished. She seemed genuinely glad to see me. She was beset by nightmares, she said. Could I help her get some rest? I took her to a physician who sagely prescribed a change in climate, rest and a diet rich in blood and iron, gave her a prescription for sedatives, and called it a day.

You know how she looked when you saw her. The day was approaching when she would have no more blood, when life as you know it would stop and she would become like me. Somehow I couldn't take her with me without some warning, but I didn't know how to do it. You see, since I was an innocent victim myself, I could speak, could warn my intended victim, because although my soul had all but died, there was still a spark that evil hadn't touched. I knew she would think it a joke if I told her about myself without warning.

Then, happily for me, you came along. I knew you would sense something amiss and I didn't care. I was almost certain of her love, and I decided to seize the few minutes left me and devil take the hindmost! When you told her to confront me, you gave me the happiest days of my life. For this I thank you sincerely. For what I have done and will ask you to do, forgive me!

Maria asked me directly, as you had known she would. I replied frankly, sparing her nothing. I told her that the fact that this life had been wished on me, as it were, gave me some rights, and that I could tell her how to rid herself of me, if she wished. Then she turned to me, her large, lovely eyes thoughtful.

"Tod, dearest," she said softly, "I must die some day, really die, so what difference does it make when? I only know that I love you. Why wait until I'm decrepit and alone, with only a few memories to look back on? Why not now, with you, where life doesn't really stop? With all I've read about this, don't you think I could free myself if I wished?"

I still wonder if she really believed me. We were married three days later. I never told her what her life with me would be like—that one day I would desert her, fearing and hating her rivalry for the very source of my life, and the ghastly chain would continue. I couldn't. I loved her so, Morris, can you understand that? I couldn't betray her then and I can't now.

On the second night of our marriage, she died as you know it, in my arms. I don't think she knows it yet. But it won't be long until she does discover it. We were quite alive when you found us; she was in an hypnotic state induced by her condition. She heard and saw nothing. But I knew. And I must keep my faith. I must, and you are the only one who can help me.

If you will show this to a priest, he will gladly accompany you to the place in Konigstein, *where we rest during the morning in a new "bed" I had specially constructed for us. I couldn't bring Maria to that other bed of corruption. A map of how to get there is enclosed. There you will perform the ancient, effective rites, and you will lay us to rest together, as we wish. That is all I ask…*

When I had finished reading I stared at nothing, trying to force myself to think. This was "all" he asked. In substance, he wished me to murder the girl I loved. I could refuse; I could ignore his request. I could even doubt the verity of his statements. He might be a madman. But I didn't doubt. I believed every word, and I knew I would do as he asked.

That she had gone willingly I didn't doubt. I no longer hated him so much; rather I pitied him, the hapless victim of a horrible chain of circumstance.

I found the priest, a venerable, gentle soul, after much searching. The younger men had looked at me searchingly, laughed and told me to read the Good Book for consolation, and to lay off the bottle. Father Kalman was understanding, with the wisdom of the very old.

"Yes, my son," he said. "I will go. Many might doubt, but I believe. Lucifer roams the earth in many guises and must be recognized and exorcised."

It was five o'clock in the morning when we approached the mausoleum. The Good Father explained that the "creatures of darkness" had to be back in their resting places before the cock crew. At night they drew sustenance; during the morning they slept.

There was a gleaming copper casket. Tod had not lied. We approached it warily. In it was nothing but grisly remains, bloodstains and dust. We drew back, fearful. Then we saw the other, newer casket in richest mahogany, almost twice the width of the copper box: *Their bridal bed!*

They lay together, his arm about her. She wore a gown of palest blue, but oh, that mockery of a gown! Stained it was with fresh blood which had seeped onto it from him. Obviously she had not taken to prowling yet. His mouth was dark, rich with blood, slightly open in a half-smile. His hand pressed her fair head close to his chest. She lay trustingly within the circle of his arm, like a small child. The priest crossed himself. The bodies twitched slightly.

"You know what you must do," Father Kalman whispered.

I nodded, the pit of my stomach churning madly. I couldn't do it! Not Maria, the lovely. But I knew I would; I had to. She must not wake again to see that blood-stained gown or to wonder at her husband's gory lips. She should know rest, eternal rest.

Father Kalman circled the box several times, ringing his small bell, and at one point laid a crucifix upon each of their chests. Their faces writhed and I felt my skin creep.

Then, chanting in a low, firm voice, the priest gave me the signal. Together we drove two long stakes, dipped first in Holy Water, home, piercing their hearts simultaneously.

The bodies leapt forward in the box, straining against the stake, and a horrible, drawn-out wail shattered the stillness of the tomb. The priest dropped to his knees and I clapped my hands over my ears, but the dreadful shriek penetrated. My stomach turned over and I retched. The Good Father followed suit. We were no supermen and our bodies and our very souls revolted against this monstrous thing.

"Let us finish, my son," the priest said slowly, after a time, his face the color of ashes. "We must bury these dead that they may sleep in consecrated ground."

I couldn't. I had to see her again before it was done. She lay, small and fragile as ever, her face calm, only there was no trace of life now. She was still and white, as only the dead—the truly dead—are. Tod's arm was flung across her chest, as if to protect her. I made myself move the arm, resting her head upon his shoulder, where it belonged. Then, as I looked, there was just Maria. Tod was gone and only a handful of dust lay piled up around the stake. It was enough. I slammed the lid shut.

Looking back now, I can see it was all for the best. Ria was different—apart from other women. A dreamer, a mystic, too easily influenced by the bizarre and un-normal. I, on the other hand, am practical almost to a fault. Had she married me I might have crushed in her the very thing that drew me to her. In time she might have grown to hate me.

Hunter, on the other hand, was a student. Introspective, given to romanticizing. Susceptible to suggestion. Had I been confronted with an Eve, I should have run like hell. To him, though, she was cloaked in mystery; hence, more desirable. What better choice for him ultimately than Ria? That Ria had to die to achieve her happiness is of no real importance. Life is a transitory thing anyway.

Sometimes, though, when I look at Ria's picture, it's hard to be practical. She was everything I shall ever want.

I had never been to Europe before the summer of 1947. I went to find Maria, to marry her. Instead, I found and murdered her, and I will never go back again.

THE END

If you've enjoyed this book, you will not want to miss these terrific titles…

ARMCHAIR SCI-FI, FANTASY, & HORROR DOUBLE NOVELS, $12.95 each

D-41 **FULL CYCLE** by Clifford D. Simak
IT WAS THE DAY OF THE ROBOT by Frank Belknap Long

D-42 **THIS CROWDED EARTH** by Robert Bloch
REIGN OF THE TELEPUPPETS by Daniel Galouye

D-43 **THE CRISPIN AFFAIR** by Jack Sharkey
THE RED HELL OF JUPITER by Paul Ernst

D-44 **PLANET OF DREAD** by Dwight V. Swain
WE THE MACHINE by Gerald Vance

D-45 **THE STAR HUNTER** by Edmond Hamilton
THE ALIEN by Raymond F. Jones

D-46 **WORLD OF IF** by Rog Phillips
SLAVE RAIDERS FROM MERCURY by Don Wilcox

D-47 **THE ULTIMATE PERIL** by Robert Abernathy
PLANET OF SHAME by Bruce Elliot

D-48 **THE FLYING EYES** by J. Hunter Holly
SOME FABULOUS YONDER by Phillip Jose Farmer

D-49 **THE COSMIC BUNGLARS** by Geoff St. Reynard
THE BUTTONED SKY by Geoff St. Reynard

D-50 **TYRANTS OF TIME** by Milton Lesser
PARIAH PLANET by Murray Leinster

ARMCHAIR SCIENCE FICTION CLASSICS, $12.95 each

C-13 **SUNKEN WORLD**
by Stanton A. Coblentz

C-14 **THE LAST VIAL**
by Sam McClatchie, M. D.

C-15 **WE WHO SURVIVED (THE FIFTH ICE AGE)**
by Sterling Noel

ARMCHAIR MASTERS OF SCIENCE FICTION SERIES, $16.95 each

MS-5 **MASTERS OF SCIENCE FICTION, Vol. Five**
Winston K. Marks—Test Colony and other tales

MS-6 **MASTERS OF SCIENCE FICTION, Vol. Six**
Fritz Leiber—Deadly Moon and other tales

If you've enjoyed this book, you will not want to miss these terrific titles…

ARMCHAIR SCI-FI & HORROR DOUBLE NOVELS, $12.95 each

D-61 **THE MAN WHO STOPPED AT NOTHING** by Paul W. Fairman
TEN FROM INFINITY by Ivar Jorgensen

D-62 **WORLDS WITHIN** by Rog Phillips
THE SLAVE by C.M. Kornbluth

D-63 **SECRET OF THE BLACK PLANET** by Milton Lesser
THE OUTCASTS OF SOLAR III by Emmett McDowell

D-64 **WEB OF THE WORLDS** by Harry Harrison and Katherine MacLean
RULE GOLDEN by Damon Knight

D-65 **TEN TO THE STARS** by Raymond Z. Gallun
THE CONQUERORS by David H. Keller, M. D.

D-66 **THE HORDE FROM INFINITY** by Dwight V. Swain
THE DAY THE EARTH FROZE by Gerald Hatch

D-67 **THE WAR OF THE WORLDS** by H. G. Wells
THE TIME MACHINE by H. G. Wells

D-68 **STARCOMBERS** by Edmond Hamilton
THE YEAR WHEN STARDUST FELL by Raymond F. Jones

D-69 **HOCUS-POCUS UNIVERSE** by Jack Williamson
QUEEN OF THE PANTHER WORLD by Berkeley Livingston

D-70 **BATTERING RAMS OF SPACE** by Don Wilcox
DOOMSDAY WING by George H. Smith

ARMCHAIR SCIENCE FICTION & FANTASY CLASSICS, $12.95 each

C-19 **EMPIRE OF JEGGA**
by David V. Reed

C-20 **THE TOMORROW PEOPLE**
by Judith Merril

C-21 **THE MAN FROM YESTERDAY**
by Howard Browne as by Lee Francis

C-22 **THE TIME TRADERS**
by Andre Norton

C-23 **ISLANDS OF SPACE**
by John W. Campbell

C-24 **THE GALAXY PRIMES**
by E. E. "Doc" Smith

If you've enjoyed this book, you will not want to miss these terrific titles...

ARMCHAIR SCI-FI & HORROR DOUBLE NOVELS, $12.95 each

ARMCHAIR SCIENCE FICTION CLASSICS, $12.95 each

ARMCHAIR SCIENCE FICTION & HORROR GEMS SERIES, $12.95 each